A BRIDGE *in* DARKNESS

Carlos Victoria

Translation from *Spanish*
by David Landau

Pureplay Press
Los Angeles

Please direct all correspondence to: editor@pureplaypress.com / Pureplay Press, 11353 Missouri Ave., Los Angeles, CA 90025.

Cataloguing-in-Publication Data
Victoria, Carlos.
    [*Puente en la oscuridad.* English]
    A bridge in darkness : a novel / by Carlos Victoria : translation to English by David Landau. — 1st English language ed.
        p. cm.
ISBN 0-9714366-4-9
1. Exiles — Florida — Miami — Fiction. 2. Persian Gulf War, 1991 — Fiction. I. Title
863.64—dc22

Library of Congress Control Number: 2003113575

Illustration: *Niño y mariposa* by Remedios Varo (oil on masonite, 1961); reproduction courtesy of the Museo de Arte Moderno de México

Author photo: Pedro Portal

Cover and book design by Wakeford Gong

Printed in the United States

Was it a vision, or a waking dream?

—John Keats

For Eduardo Fajardo and Lourdes Tomás

A BRIDGE IN DARKNESS

ONE

At age thirty-nine, Natán Velázquez found out he had a half-brother.

"I have a brother," he told himself, purposely omitting the word "half," which he found a limitation. An only child, he had forever wanted to share the mystery, or at times the shame, of having parents. Reuniting with his brother, he imagined, would be like facing a lost fragment of mirror: finding in another person the identical mole on the right hand, that same inflection in the voice, the same way of knitting one's eyebrow or glancing sideways. Even more, he could count on a companion for life's inexorable stretches; a confidant, a shoulder to lean on during a lonely turn. Natán was a man given to fantasy, a man who in another time—say, a century ago—might have written poetry.

Now he was just a dreamer with no family ties, no kids, no wife, no homeland—hiding from life in his daily routine at a Miami export company that sent tanker parts to Venezuela. His apartment had a balcony overlooking a lake that reflected, at nightfall, a forest of pines on the opposite shore and gave the fleeting impression that life repeats itself down to the last detail, an idea that made him secure and also disquieted him. At times a breeze rippling the water broke the stillness of the reflection, tossed a small boat near a ramshackle dock, stirred branches that raised themselves like arms to touch the edges of his quiet balcony, or frightened a bird of sinister plumage that flew off with a squawk into the grove of pines. The bird cast a shadow over the tiny waves before vanishing into the foliage; its lyrical moans echoed through the vegetation. Then the humid air made a mist on the glass of his sliding door and the landscape faded away, overcome by the invading dark. The living-room lamp shone on the glass where water drops had formed arabesques, indefinite figures. Natán felt unhappy with his present situation, while his past had grown distant from him.

Here, however, was his father's letter, dated with a trembling hand in the city of Camagüey, where Natán once had sauntered about on streets paved with cobblestones, a backward youth unable to give his all to the passions of life, whether to sex, to riches, to the hurly-burly of politics or the quest for power. His father, quite the opposite, had been a slave to those excesses that parade under handsome names: love, justice, the general welfare, equality, discipline, heroism. To those pursuits, Father had dedicated his energetic body and a soul that wavered between reality and fantasy, tinged with an endemic dose of cruelty; because, or so Natán imagined, a man like his father—a womanizer, a coveter, a doctrinaire socialist who abused his underlings—could never be the good-natured person he pretended or fancied himself to be. And now this unsteady letter pointed to other feelings in the old man: uncertainty and guilt.

"I never wanted to tell you, but you've got a brother—a bit older than you, just two or three months, maybe four. I haven't seen him since he was a boy. He went to the States with his mother. Now that your mother has died—I never told her, I didn't want to give her that shame, I gave her plenty before the divorce—I think you should look for him. I hear he also lives in Miami. I have no way of knowing where he is. You can try to find his aunt, his mother's sister. Years ago she wrote and asked me to do something for a cousin in jail here. The lady's name is Alicia Lastre. I don't know if she still has the same address and phone number, but anyway here they are...."

The rest of the letter was drenched in political diatribes that Natán knew by heart. On this occasion they sounded more like a defense than a reproach, maybe because their ideology had fallen into disgrace all over the world, or maybe because the writer, a functionary in Cuba's communist regime who had a son—or two— in exile, now found himself at death's door; for in his last letter a few months earlier, the old man had said the doctor gave him little time to live. Though he hadn't mentioned an actual illness, it seemed his heart or liver or some other vital organ had fatally weakened; and seventy years of passionate intensity were now pointing to their pitiless conclusion.

Sitting on his darkened balcony, Natán looked out at the faraway lights of downtown Miami and thought about his father, who would soon die; about his mother, whom he had buried in Florida, an old emigrant lady interred in a country she had never managed to understand; and the lake's inky-black waters, headlights on the highway, songs of nighttime birds, planes taking off at the airport nearby, shadows of pine trees on a deserted shore led him to reflect on death, solitude, exile, and the unaccountable truth of being alive.

Neither the lively images from his television set, where all manner of melodrama or foolish comedy unfolded, nor the occasional visits of his two lovers—Sandra the divorcée or Teresa his neighbor, a married woman with two daughters—could stir in him even the tiniest excitement that people need for any pleasure in life.

Every day, Monday to Saturday, he plunged into the dreary world of commerce, where prices, motor serial numbers, and piece counts went back and forth over the phone. Faceless voices in different accents and languages pronounced the same vacant courtesies. With a businessman's cool dexterity, Natán worked the invisible net that connected Miami to San Francisco, New York, Chicago, Houston, Caracas and Maracaibo. The boss had been happy enough with him to give him a brand new car. And with his commission from a recent sale, he had made the down payment on his apartment by the lake. He alone knew that his businessman's identity was a sham. Inside himself he felt unworthy, unsure, unhappy; and he was pushing forty.

"So it seems I have a brother," he mused aloud on reading his father's letter.

That night he clumsily delivered the news to Sandra, who burst out laughing.

"Don't expect too much! I've got five," she said.

They had sex on the carpet, Natán leading her to different positions in order to fend off the boredom he had started to feel with her anxious, overripe body—a body that pursued him at every instant. Sandra had wanted to do it with the lights on, maybe so she could read her lover's face during the act. Natán wanted to unload the woman and didn't know how. He only understood the moment had come for the two of them to set up house together or break it off. Sandra was tired of living alone. Her son had left with his father, and she didn't want to go through life as someone's sweetheart. She was also possessive, and she suspected Natán was seeing someone else.

"I need more time," he said. "We should know each other better."

"More time? Ten months isn't enough? I'm thirty-five, you're almost forty. We're not kids anymore."

"That's just it, Sandra. What's ten months? Nothing."

When they were done on the floor, Natán, irascible and panting for air, opened the balcony door. The apartment became small when Sandra went walking around barefoot from room to room, fixing her hair, drying off drops that slithered on her flesh after a shower, criticizing his mess of clothes or books and, worst of all, trying to pick up the scent of his other visitor. Her own perfume stuck to the towels and furniture with a dogged insistence. She already behaved like mistress of the house. She wanted to bear Natán's child.

"It's time for you to think about being a father," Sandra told him that night.

"I'm not cut out for having children," he answered. "I'll never be a good father. My father wasn't. These things are hereditary. And if I think about what's happened to my brother, even I can't complain."

"Your half-brother," Sandra corrected him.

"Yes, half—you're right—my half-brother. My father says his name is José."

A man called José Velázquez. A disembodied being. Mustachioed or clean-shaven. A full head of hair or a bowling ball. A smiling expression or a sneering one. An ordinary guy or an illustrious professor. A dedicated worker or a goof-off. A family man or a stubborn old bachelor like himself. A model of balance or a nut case. A fugitive from the law or a judge. An atheist or a pastor. Quick to anger or easygoing, friendly or vindictive, serious or a clown, honorable or a liar, clumsy or deft, with a sunny disposition or a remorseless one. José Velázquez. Yes, Natán reflected, names are empty of meaning; and his half-brother's name was no exception.

The telephone, a device that at times determines the course of things, a minor deity in the service of Fate—a tamed and "technified" Hermes, Natán mused in recalling his high-school study of Greek—now put him in contact with the lady his father had mentioned.

"Alicia Lastre?" Natán asked in a nervous voice. "Are you the aunt of José Velázquez?"

Yes, she was. She spoke in the deliberate, dispassionate tone of someone for whom life holds no further surprises. Months had passed since she had heard anything of her nephew, who came and went without notice—a wanderer who showed up on the spur of the moment and departed just as unexpectedly, with an abrupt and puzzling farewell, never spelling out his plans, not wanting to give others a way of finding him.

He could be anywhere, Alicia said. One time he had sent her a postcard with a date-stamp from Argentina. His trade was unknown, maybe because he had none. Alicia had gotten to meet several of his lovers who had called her, politely inquired about her health or welfare, and after some minutes of mindless chatter, with poorly feigned disinterest, asked after José. He also had a few friends who apparently held him in high esteem but always wound up bemoaning his shiftiness, his unsteady, evasive nature.

Natán decided to pay Alicia a visit. The elderly lady lived in a tumbledown building in the poorest part of Little Havana. The trees, in accord with the houses, were depressed and rickety structures, at times concealing, with their threadbare foliage, the progressive erosion of walls and roofs. Natán entered the former hotel, now a lodging for pensioners, with the embarrassment of an inopportune visitor. The stairway stank of cats' urine. The carpet had all but disappeared under layers of filth; but Alicia's apartment, overstuffed with furniture and knickknacks, was apparently immune from dust and gave off a seasoned elegance. The octogenarian with a worshipper's gaze wore a spotless white dress, and her hands had a youthful sheen. Her gestures were informal, without ever missing their measure of courtesy. However, the light suffusing the room disturbed him. It seemed to come from several windows, raising slivers of color through the jam-packed dwelling; but the windows were actually shuttered, and the center of the room was lit with a single white lamp that overpowered the faint glow of candles on an altar fixed to the wall.

After a bit of small talk about ailments that older people use to chat up a stranger, the lady said quite unexpectedly, "José often spoke about you."

"About me?" Natán asked in astonishment. "He knew who I was?"

"Of course. He saw you several times in Cuba and then here, when you came—ten years ago, isn't it? I remember him telling me: My brother has arrived. I even asked him to bring you around, but he never answered me. That was just like him. And I didn't press him. It was at the time his mother died—may she rest in peace. Thanks to her, I got out of the hell that Cuba has become."

"No! Not possible. He must have been talking about another brother."

"Another brother? No, he's an only child on his mother's side, as you are. As far as I understand, your father had no other children—or none that anybody knew. José's mother never married after her fiasco with your father. When he met her she was a virgin, and he was the only man of her life. It seems your father had this mysterious power with women. He left his mark on them. I pray to God that He forgive your father the harm he has done. He's not bad in his heart; he did me a great favor some years ago. He interceded for a cousin of mine who was a prisoner in Cuba."

"Why did José never approach me? Why didn't he tell me who he was? Did he say he had spoken with me?"

"Not really. A number of times he came and told me: Today I saw my brother. And then he started in about something else. I don't ask him questions because José has always been a bit odd, reserved about his own affairs, too reserved, just like his mother, may she rest in peace. He got this trait from her. It's how he is. No one knows what he thinks. He tells you what he wants to tell you, and not another word."

"Do you have a photo of him?"

"I don't think so. He didn't like being photographed, any more than his mother did. From boyhood he had a phobia about that. I, on the other hand, being quite photogenic and also vain—why deny it—I've got a tremendous photo collection, hundreds of photos. Too bad, many of them are back in Cuba. Photos are good for showing other people how you used to be; because, my son, you change, you change until you become unrecognizable, and people don't want to think you were any other way. Even José has changed so much, he was such a handsome fellow, in a way he still is, but if you saw him now—he's gone white-haired, not a dark strand on his head. José has suffered greatly."

"We've all suffered," Natán said in a cutting tone, and he was taken aback by his own aggressiveness.

"That's true," the old lady hurried to agree. "All of us do that, all of us—from rich to poor, young to old—but José suffers more because he holds his suffering inside. He talks about this or that, but not about his own problems. I've never heard him complain. José is a saint, do you see? Some women have told me horror stories about him, but I know it's out of spite."

They heard a frenzied scratching of claws at the window. Across the lady's face, lit up by a gentle beam of the remarkable light shining in the room—which Natán supposed must be coming from a skylight, though he didn't look up for fear of being unseemly— there passed a slight shadow of irritation.

"It's the cat on the balcony," she said, "but we won't let him come in. He's behaved very badly, very badly. We're punishing him. What was I saying? Oh yes, those women in love with my nephew José."

"If you could give me a phone number, maybe through one of those ladies... Please understand, I want to know him. After all, he's my only brother—but how bizarre it is that he has never contacted me, even knowing who I am! He probably hates me."

Alicia Lastre bared her gums.

"José, hate? It's obvious you don't know him. José is love itself, love through and through. But he's always wanted to be free. Even from his mother, whom he adored. So I think you'd only lose time talking to those women—but maybe I have some numbers—yes, even if I haven't spoken with any of them for some time now—a certain Gladys, who used to ring me up quite a lot, and another called La China—also a friend, Gabriel Perdomo, who passed by here a couple of times—so many names, my son, so many people! I've known so many people, in Cuba and over here. It's like a dream, or maybe a nightmare. Time passes, people come and go, a lot of them die. Can I make you some coffee?"

Natán left the building at dusk. For a moment he hesitated, uncertain; he couldn't remember where he'd left the car. He was afraid someone might have stolen it, since the area gave off a sinister feeling in the half-light of day's end. In a doorway, a trio of ragged men drinking beer, their mouths attached to the flimsy metal cans, went silent as he passed. At the corner, young guys with marked Hispanic profiles were whispering under a street lamp. Their surly faces promised violence and their bodies gave off an acrid odor so strong as to be unnatural. Then he saw his car sitting defenseless at the opposite curb, near a cafeteria that exuded the stench of rotten lard. In another doorway a gaggle of Cubans—no mistaking their abrupt manner of speech—were making an uproar about the double-dealing of international politics, their voices eclipsing another, also distinctly Cuban, that jabbered from the radio.

A transplanted people, Natán thought as he languidly opened his car door—a graft that doesn't take. He and his brother had become denizens of that artificial world: a people who didn't fit in their own country or in any other.

As he started the engine, a car behind him peeled out with a big noise. Natán wanted the other car to pass him, but the other, its windows darkened, gave him the right of way. Natán turned at the corner, then at the next and the one after that. In the unrevealing semidarkness, the streets looked the same. On the rundown sidewalks, he found transients whose miserable appearance discouraged him from asking for the directions he needed. He was about to turn into a blind alley that ended at the river when the shadow of an enormous ship hulking in the water gave him pause. He was lost. He saw in the rearview mirror that the same car was following him closely, with its lights turned off. The car's windows, almost completely black, gave no view of the driver. It must be a coincidence, he told himself; but after driving several blocks with no particular aim, and realizing the darkened car hadn't stopped following him, he halted and got out. Moving away from his door with a slight grimace, he went toward the other car, which had also stopped in the middle of the empty street.

Night had closed in. He contrived to walk with the brazen and energetic step he'd seen in B-films and TV dramas, groping blatantly in his pocket to pretend he was carrying a pistol. As Natán approached, the car pulled back slowly, spun around and quickly made off, throwing up a toxic cloud that dissolved in the dark and sickly trees. In the car's rapid retreat, Natán had barely made out the driver's profile through the half-open front window.

Amid the shadows, all he had seen clearly was a man with white hair.

CHAPTER
TWO

Mercedes Suárez, also known as "La China," inhabited the make-believe world of seamstresses. The clothing factory where she contorted her fingers to earn a livelihood seemed to her as unreal as her father's house, where she shared a room with her twelve-year-old boy, and suffered a stepmother's rudeness along with an uncle's drinking bouts. Mercedes nourished her soul with TV melodramas, dreams of winning the lottery—whose tickets grew faded and wrinkled at the bottoms of her overstuffed drawers—and advertisements promising a brilliant future to anyone who mastered English, a language beyond her grasp; for, coming to the States at age twenty-three, Mercedes could barely count on the rudiments of her own fractured Spanish, a legacy of her Cuban peasant family's whimsical speech. The magic tube in the corner of her bedroom, shimmering with colors, filled her dreams with heartening apparitions, with impetuous, effervescent images—and when she pressed the button to snuff out the make-believe world, its afterglow played on the wall, for hours, above the head of her sleeping child.

José had been part and parcel of the dream. He'd never promised marriage, but he did have a special gift for soothing her boy. José used to crawl on the floor so the boy could jump up and ride him horseback. Overcome with excitement, the boy clapped his shoulder, yanked his hair and kicked heels into his ribs. On Sundays, José took the boy to the beach at Key Biscayne and taught him to swim while mom listened to popular singers on the radio, just closing her eyes and giving herself up to sinuous melodies under a broiling sun. They were together for a summer. At the time, José drove a rig or maybe a taxi or, as Mercedes good-humoredly recalled, something that moved. He never exactly explained what he did for a living, as if that had nothing to do with his role as her lover; as if the particulars of his work day were as private a matter as changing underwear. He seemed to be stable, but he was a gambler: *jai alai,* horses, dog races. He was obsessed with chance and numerology, trying to recast his life and the lives of those he loved by playing with numbers. According to Mercedes, he had a huge capacity for love, just as his aunt Alicia had said.

Something went missing, for chance declined to go along with him. To Mercedes, it hardly mattered. Her own life was a babbling brook of fantasies: a stream of colors and sounds that would one day run across her threshold and take shape as happiness incarnate. José, however, was not a happy man. Once, while he was cutting his toenails, he said he was thinking about ways to kill himself. At other times he spoke about bringing freedom to Cuba. He wanted to do something really big, or nothing at all. Then he stopped calling her, and someone told Mercedes he had gotten himself another woman.

"I have no bad feelings for him," she told Natán as they sat at the end of a park bench where they had met by appointment. The hem of her skirt lay gently on the wooden slats, and an afternoon's quiet wafted over them both. "He was a very good man. He just couldn't control himself."

Gladys was a different story. She gave the impression of having her feet on the ground. A dead husband—maybe a drug dealer, Natán thought—had willed her a house in Coral Gables and money enough to open a hair salon. Her hands and neck weighed down with jewelry, she greeted Natán in the office of her salon with a derisive courtesy and the sort of hardened expression that wealth can give to people. The mingled perfumes of shampoos, creams and lotions cut into Natán's breath. The lady's own hairdo, thick and shiny with a dark blue tinge, made a man want to touch it, or even to nibble at some of the strands; but of the two women who had been involved with his brother José, Natán preferred the hapless dreamer Mercedes.

"My husband brought him to the house. They were in business together. I think José was selling used cars for commission, but I'm not sure. Once I went with the two of them to an automobile auction in Fort Lauderdale. When my husband died—someone killed him with a bullet, it was an accident, really terrible, the shooter must have mistaken him for someone else—José was with him, he also got wounded but it was nothing, a scratch on his arm or shoulder, as far as I heard. And I, as you can imagine, went through the worst time of my life. We never managed to have children, though we had always been trying. And my whole family was in Cuba."

"How long ago was that?" Natán asked.

"Seven years, nearly seven since Adolfo died. I was quite alone. As you can imagine, my nerves were in ruins. José started dropping by, we passed the time talking about Adolfo, and sometimes he took me out to a restaurant. José had always shown me respect, he was very courteous, but something was there, I don't know, he had something in him I didn't like. I'm sorry for using this word about your brother, but he had something abnormal in him. You got the idea he wasn't completely sincere. That's not it, exactly; he seemed to be hiding something—I don't know—but as I say, I was very alone, and he never took liberties with me, not even indirectly—understand? And besides, he was the last person to see my husband alive, because Adolfo died almost in an instant. The poor man didn't even make it to the hospital. The killer got away in a car. To this day no one knows who he was. If Adolfo had been another kind of man—I mean, if he had been a politician or a policeman or someone with influence, I'm quite sure...."

Just then a lady opened the door and said in the apprehensive tone of an employee speaking to a boss: "A vendor wants to know if you'll be much longer."

The jewel-heavy hands jingled with annoyance; red nails, filed like little knives, made ominous circles in the fragrant air.

"I said quite clearly I was not to be interrupted, not even for phone calls. Tell him that if he's in such a hurry he should just go. Tell him exactly like that."

"I don't want to intrude," Natán said.

"It's not your fault. I can't speak in peace, even in my own shop. Anyway, the thing is that José came around to my house. I was depressed, he was good company for me. Then people started talking—you know, neighbors and friends, or so-called friends—of course you understand what I'm saying. *Anyway,*" she said, pronouncing that word in English, "I've never gone along with what most people say, I've always been quite independent, not a feminist or a defender of causes or a political activist, nothing of the sort, but very aware of my rights, of my individuality, and I just didn't care what people said about me."

"How is my brother abnormal?" Natán asked.

Gladys took up a pen and started scribbling on a piece of paper.

"I can't really tell you. He was a man who spoke in code, a quiet man who never said anything about himself or his life; and if anyone asked questions he sidestepped them, or answered by telling a story that had nothing to do with what the person was asking. I never knew where he lived or anything about his family. I heard about his aunt by sheer accident. He was always helpful, I'll give him that, but when you needed him most he didn't show up, and months went by without a call; well then, a complicated man, probably a little scatterbrained, intelligent but in an odd way. I always showed him friendship, I always made clear that it was friendship and nothing more—understand? And after all, I don't know, he gave me the impression he was going off to look for something else, or maybe he was trying to scare something out of me. I don't know."

"His aunt told me the two of you became intimate," Natán said.

Gladys tossed her hair in laughter, then proceeded to restore the fancy hairdo.

"Oh, that old lady! I never told her anything and I'm sure José didn't, either; but look, you're his brother, you don't know him, you're looking for him, and you seem to be a serious, reliable person. To speak frankly, after some time had gone by, I mean, a lot of time after Adolfo's death, it's true, something happened, it was an impulse. As I'm telling you, I was very alone, but José is not a man to give himself to other people. Or maybe I should say he gives himself to people in *his* way, and he also wants people to give themselves in his way—understand? Let's say we spent a weekend together and then he was off. Later he came back, saying things I didn't follow about punishments and rewards, telling all kinds of stories, breaking off in the middle of sentences. I'm a normal person, very normal, I got out of Cuba with my husband twenty years ago and left my whole family behind, and then I had the shame of becoming a widow in this country, but despite everything I've moved forward because I'm strong and I've got will power and I think carefully before I make decisions—understand?—but sometimes you make a mistake, and I made a mistake with José. With someone like him, you don't want to get too close. I could tell you some unpleasant things, but what's the use? A friend told me she'd heard he was dead, and I don't like to talk about dead people; but a good while afterward I heard someone had seen him about a year earlier. He likes to wrap himself in mystery, probably to give himself an extra interest. He might even be in jail. Who knows? Under the mask of kindness people saw in him, and I saw it too, he was the most self-centered man in the universe. He was self-centered enough to kill, and God forgive me if that's a slander. My advice, if advice is what you want, is to forget him. You say that until a few days ago you didn't know you had a brother. So why not just go on as if you didn't have one? I haven't seen José for three years, and let me tell you, those have been the three easiest years I've had since Adolfo died. And now I'll excuse myself, because I've got a lot of things to do. You don't know what it is to have a business. It makes you crazy."

Gladys, however, hadn't yet finished.

"José said he considered himself a spiritual man," she said, taking up the pen once more and scribbling the paper full of flowery signatures, "although I never heard him talk about religion. And in his way he let me know that my concern with money annoyed him, but he gambled everything he earned. And doesn't one gamble in order to get more? Answer me that. He's looking for fame and power like everyone else, but since he's not straightforward he goes about it differently. I, for my part, am not a hypocrite. What did you say your name was?"

"Natán Velázquez. He never talked about me?"

"Never. My impression was that he despised his family—but maybe I'm mistaken."

"Thank you," Natán said.

That night he dreamt of Mercedes and Gladys arguing over a glass figurine, a strangely shaped decoration that looked like a kneeling idol, rather hideous, with shortened arms and a flattened head. Mesmerized by this combat which had sprung up in his own living room, Natán was slowly sipping an unfiltered wine that burned his tongue and throat. The two women hurled ferocious insults at each other. One of them abruptly let the figurine drop; it hit the flagstone floor and shattered to smithereens. A young boy with painted lips came through the balcony door. With great deliberation he began to pick up the shards of glass. At that instant Natán awoke.

As the day wore on, and he tried to close a deal with the owner of a tuna fishing fleet, he was surprised to see—never having believed in the revelatory power of dreams—that the nightmare had borne him a message. His attempt to get close to his brother by means of those women was utterly useless. Neither Mercedes nor Gladys had anything to offer him.

So he resolved to forget them.

CHAPTER

THREE

Voices took over Natán's life. Neither strong nor well defined, they grew intrusive when he put head to pillow. Keenly feminine, brusquely masculine or childishly neutral, they interwove phrases in English and Spanish or, in the Miami manner, piled words from both languages helter-skelter on top of each other—an improbable sound for anyone who has lived in a place where language is always the same, one and indivisible.

The fragments he heard had no definite meaning. They were pieces of verbiage you would scarcely comprehend if they came to you by chance, like snippets from a radio being switched from one station to another.

His neighbor Teresa sometimes took advantage of her husband's absence to leave her daughters with their grandmother and spend half an hour in Natán's bed. They moaned and groped without speaking a word, two bodies immersed in the ardent struggle for possession and recognition—bathed in sweat, overcome by swollen parts of themselves that clamored for attention, facing a lit-up TV screen that Natán had muted. Voiceless faces tried to give them a piece of advice, a news bulletin of pressing importance, pointers for living or cooking or simply a popular song; but the lips moved in vain. The woman gave herself to him, convulsing, in the semidarkness of noon become night by the grace of drawn curtains. Afterward Teresa got dressed in sorrow and shame. Her youthful innocence lost more luster with every motion. Jarring steps in the hallway caught her by surprise and etched on her face a grimace of alarm that concealed itself under an opportune cascade of hair. At times she went off without saying goodbye. Whenever she did that, Natán imagined she was telling herself not to go back to him. A half-hour of delight and oblivion could not repay the guilt. She would start by getting something nice for her husband, like a tool kit. Then, surely, they would be taking their girls to the movies on Sunday afternoon; and in time she would forget her indolent lover who smoked in the nude as he gazed at the ceiling.

But after three days or more—one time he had had to wait a month—she would reappear without fanfare at his door. Natán was always happy to see her. After his fashion, he loved her.

"Teresa, I've found out I have a brother."

She told him to look in the phone book. How could so simple an idea not have occurred to him? The book listed several men in the Miami area with the name José Velázquez. The first of these Natán recognized as a Mexican by his particular signoff; the man put an end to Natán's unsteady hope with a crisp and cordial "*Mande.*" The second José, an old man from Santiago de Cuba, regaled the telephone visitor with his entire life story, whose only point of interest was that, as the result of a youthful accident, the man had passed through life as a cripple. Natán patiently heard the compact chronicle of seven deadly boring decades whose undoubted treasure had been six children and seventeen grandchildren. José Velázquez number three, a gynecologist with a wicked sense of humor, pretended at first to be the man Natán was trying to find, claiming to believe, or so he said afterward, that the call had been a joke. After apologizing, the man told a few jokes about Fidel Castro and lamented the high cost of medical insurance. The fourth José had an answering machine without a recorded greeting; after the signal giving callers a chance to speak, Natán left his name and number and asked for a return call, saying it was an important matter. Lucky contestant number five was a Nicaraguan who acted uneasy and suspicious before cutting off the conversation. The sixth and final José Velázquez was a Cuban-American whose Spanish had to be heard to be believed.

On another night—after the noise that crowded Natán's head had yielded to the gentle regions of sleep—a phone call awakened him. Through the haze of slumber, he heard a woman ask: "You're the one who left a message for José Velázquez?"

"Yes, my name is Natán."

"I know. We heard your message."

"Is he there?"

"No, he's at work. He's the night watchman at an apartment complex in Miami Lakes. If you want to, you can go and see him after ten in the evening."

"Are you his wife?"

"No, I'm a friend. He asked me to call you because he sleeps during the day, and when he's called, you haven't answered. Here's the address."

Next night, Natán slowly drove along a dark avenue protected by trees whose quiet trunks appeared to shelter furtive spirits. Gnarled roots came snaking toward the asphalt and touched it with their tips. Unsociable garden walls concealed mansions behind them, allowing scarcely a glimpse of the roofs. It had just rained, and water from ample puddles gushed up as he drove through them, annoyingly spraying the windshield. His beams made only partial headway in the dense blackness around the cypresses, oaks and pines. Natán twice got out of the car to check house numbers. At last he saw, fashioned in cement with ludicrous decoration, the words *Spring Lake Village.* The building's wrought-iron gate, enfolded by luxuriant vegetation, was open. The sentry box where the watchman, a certain José Velázquez, should have been on duty was empty. A rickety chair testified to the absence of the guard. Natán looked at his watch; it was eleven-thirty.

Even if he had moderated his journey with a dose of skepticism, he had a premonition that the trip would not be in vain; for it was hardly conceivable that someone would have asked a woman to call him in the middle of the night and give this address if that someone were not Natán's brother and had not recognized his name.

He parked his car to the side of the entrance and walked aimlessly among the vehicles, whose moistened bodies glowed faintly under sallow lamplight. The makes and models denoted a middle-class population in decline, or perhaps a *petite bourgeoisie* on the rise. The building itself, no doubt, had been luxurious in its day, but slight cracks in the mosaics, a few stains on the walls and some nicks in the wooden doors revealed that its early splendor had faded away. In his youth Natán had memorized certain texts of Marx, whose fixation on class struggle and economic power had gravely marked the student's worldview. He reflected that he was no longer a youth, while Marx had become a thinker mired in an earlier epoch and scorned in the present one. Natán caught hold of himself. He had not come to this dismal place to ponder the issue of social classes, but to find a man who watched over the residents' sleep.

Just then a woman came out of her apartment with a dog that needed to do its business.

"Good evening," Natán said in English. "I am looking for the security guard."

"Security guard?" the woman said in an odd, throaty accent, while her eyes mistrusted him. "There's no security guard here."

Which could mean they had no guard, or perhaps he wasn't there now. Natán began to wander through a labyrinth of opaque passageways, to stroll through the enormous parking lot and range over side-paths, until at once he found himself in front of a lake where the sound of insects only deepened the silence. A fish jumped about in the water near a dock in ruins. Drawing close to a bank festooned in grasses, Natán had the fleeting impression that this was the lake next to his home, and that in truth he had only come down from his apartment to stroll along the water, as he was wont to do on his insomniac nights. The vivid sensation gripped him with fear, as if he were in an ambush.

On the other shore, in a row of pines like the one facing his balcony, a nocturnal bird was sobbing. Natán thought he saw a figure moving with care among the trees. He wanted to cry out "José!" and then stopped himself. It was preposterous to suppose the security guard had crossed the lake, which anyway—now that Natán had regained his senses—didn't look a whit like the one that skirted his own building.

He went back to the watchman's cabin steeped in sweat, wiping his hair as if stretching out a wrinkled fabric, and sat down on the one piece of furniture in the tiny booth. On the floor he found a handwritten paper and picked it up. The words had been smudged by moisture and dirt. In the semidarkness they were difficult to read:

> *This living hand, now warm and capable*
> *Of earnest grasping, would, if it were cold*
> *And in the icy silence of the tomb,*
> *So haunt thy days and chill thy dreaming nights*

That thou wouldst wish thine own heart dry of blood
So in my veins red life might stream again,
And thou be conscience-calmed—see here it is—
I hold it towards you.

Natán folded the paper and tucked it away in a pocket. A love poem, he told himself; awkward, somewhat sinister, vaguely familiar. A rejected man was trying to extract tenderness by means of threats. Could it be that the watchman José Velázquez also dabbled in poetry? Natán decided to wait half an hour more. Maybe the man had gone for a late supper. Natán was angry at himself for not having spoken frankly with the woman who had phoned him— or at very least, for not having asked her two or three questions that would have given a clue as to whether this José was his father's son. Just now, Natán could not think of the man as his brother or half-brother. He sat in the sentry's box, fighting off mosquitoes and a sickening sadness as a number of cars went by without stopping. One of these turned back. The driver lowered his window and asked in English, then in Spanish: "Are you waiting for someone?"

"For the security guard," Natán answered.

"I'm the manager of the building. We haven't had a security guard here for seven months. Can I help you?"

"Someone told me that a man I know works as a guard here."

"Then someone spoke incorrectly. Are you sure this is the place? Spring Lake Village?"

"Very sure. Did you say seven months?"

"Maybe more. I've been here seven months, and when I got here the place had no guard."

A drizzle beat against Natán's bedroom window all night, rebounding against pallid voices that whispered interminably and vied with each other in a nimble, tortuous concert. Half asleep,

Natán kept telling himself he had been the victim of a prank. That was the only explanation. As soon as dawn appeared, he looked in the phone book for the number of the José Velázquez—he had made identifying marks for each one—on whose line he had left a message. Natán dialed, quite ready even at that hour to demand an explanation; but instead of ringing he heard the recorded announcement that coldly tells you a number has been disconnected.

He jotted down the address of the house. That evening, after a day on the phone with people in several cities who used various idioms or forms of courtesy—after having written long, boring lists of numbers that bore no relationship to life—he plucked up his spirit to go and have it out with the pranksters.

The tenant had moved out yesterday; or so said a lady across a fence to the visitor who had been anxiously knocking at the door of a house that was obviously vacant, its uncurtained windows giving a clear view into barren rooms. No, it wasn't a white-haired man, unless he'd dyed it—which wouldn't be unheard-of in Miami, according to this woman who was quick to give her opinion—but yes, he seemed to be about forty and, according to what he had once told her, a native of Havana; a person with an erratic life, who had visits from women of doubtful virtue and men of frightening appearance, or so said the neighbor, to whom Natán explained that he was not personally acquainted with the man. The lady had been glad to see her neighbor go, because in a city as depraved as this one, with so much crime and violence and shame—God save us!—a neighbor who used drugs or sold them, or probably both, was the worst thing that could befall a person. In Cuba she would never have had such problems, but exile had obliged her to witness the lowest forms of depravity, all the fault of that accursed tyrant. At times the lady wished she were dead, but she had had to keep fighting, to keep suffering, always at risk of having dangerous people next door. Miami had become a den of criminals. Natán agreed with her.

"The man's name was José, wasn't it?" Natán asked.

"He told me his name was Ernesto, but from a man like that you can expect anything, including a false name."

Sitting on his balcony at day's end—as he looked beyond the lake, the pines and the airport's landing strip to find rows of lit-up autos thronging the highways—Natán came to the conviction that his life had become a lie. At other moments he had glimpsed the notion, he had heard about other people having it too, but now it was a physical sensation, like a wind that shook the branches near his railing and made ripples on the stagnant surface of the lake, or like something more personal—an ache, an eruption, a spasm.

First, he told himself, he should break with Sandra, because no genuine relationship could feed on sexual juggling acts, on caresses and secretions that had become a forced habit. Even Sandra would grant that he was right. After all, didn't she want from Natán precisely what he wouldn't or couldn't give—a regular life, a roof over her head, security? With Teresa, at least, he had the rudiments of mutual affection. Their shared guilt only drew them closer. They were partners in crime. And aside from those brief spells of pleasure, Teresa asked nothing of him.

Next he should quit his job; no doubt his savings would let him stay unemployed for several months. At such time as communism—or the mental illness that went by the name of communism—should reach an end in Cuba, perhaps he would go back. In the final tally, even if his bond with Cuba had diminished to become an aching mirage, the island was still his home. For the present he determined to find his brother, if only to reprove him for inconstancy.

He watched TV until dawn; watched without seeing, mechanically changing the channels, at times nodding off, at times quite alert to the bombings and murders that followed each other without pity or letup. The news also spoke about a war soon to come, repeating names of countries that for Natán were hardly more than recondite points on a map of dreams: Iraq, Kuwait, Saudi Arabia. Soldiers with gas masks were giving themselves over to ridiculous drills in the depths of the desert. Perhaps his brother was one of those soldiers who were preparing to die. Or perhaps he was the blocked-out face on a TV interview show, recounting a story of alcoholism and drug addiction, clinging to anonymity before the greedy camera which kept trying to take in his features, only returning an ominous profile, an inscrutable shadow.

As he listened, Natán recalled that he himself had once flirted with alcohol and pot; but those experiences, that entry into the whirlwind of fleeting, impassioned sensations, had only dealt him a momentary relief before unrest and frustration came back to badger him with ever greater insistence. At once he felt afraid he might give in to the impulse of throwing himself off the balcony and plunging into the lake, whose waters quietly lapped the grassy shore beneath. He had once read that death was only another lie, probably the basest lie of all. Where had he read that?

This living hand ... The lines of the poem came back to him. A hand that waited for another to grasp it; not soon, but *now*. Whoever rejected the hand would atone with pangs of conscience, or perhaps with suicide. Or with a life sentence. Or sacrifice. Or grief. Or terror. So many ways to suffer punishment; but where to find the waiting hand? The poem, he thought, had something to reveal about his own existence; *his,* Natán's. If so, what part was he playing? Was it he who held out the hand, or he who rejected it?

Time to turn off the TV, he told himself—to snuff out that

realm of false color to which women like his brother's ex-lover Mercedes were wont to attach themselves; time to rejoin the silent reality of his rooms where he could still feel Sandra's insistent perfume, and even more the ungrateful odor of a lonely man's dwelling that sooner or later needs a woman's hand to clean and freshen it, as only a woman knows how.

No sooner had the U.S. president disappeared from the TV screen in mid-phrase than Natán was standing in darkness, looking through his picture window at the night that had enveloped the lake. The planes on the airport runway looked like giant birds at rest; the stars quivered unsteadily in the rippling water.

Just before drawing the curtain that would shield him from morning's light, he thought he saw a shape wandering through the forest of pines. Perhaps a vagrant, he thought, or a hunter. Or someone who had dropped something there during the day and was trying to get it back. No sooner had the shadow paused at the edge of the water than it vanished into the trees.

At that moment it began to rain.

FOUR

Gabriel Perdomo's room had a commanding view of downtown Miami, Biscayne Bay and the islands around Miami Beach. If Natán had gotten there blindfolded, he would have thought the place a top-class hotel. Out of a picture window on an upper floor, he could enjoy those dark-glass, money-exuding skyscrapers, and a sea garlanded with fanciful ribbons of foam, as well as the glittering keys, tamed by an influx of immigrants whose hard work—or in some cases, frauds or crimes—had erected, in the space of a few decades, an elaborate complex of hotels, shops, banks and luxury dwellings.

In his journey to that aseptic room, through lobbies, elevators and austere corridors, Natán had run into hurrying nurses, unkempt stretchers, IV bottles, doctors who wore their stethoscopes like gold necklaces; and here, on the floor where Gabriel Perdomo might have looked like a guest getting the royal treatment, the cryptic stares of women who sauntered about with snuffed-out cigarettes between their lips, or the disheveled appearance of men who gazed at the ceiling with a punished child's sullen attitude, clearly stamped the place a mental ward.

Gabriel, a wizened man with a reckless expression and a tic on his mouth that seemed to bolster up his words when he spoke, greeted Natán coldly and then, like a naturalist viewing an insect, watched the visitor explain himself.

"So you say you're the brother of José Velázquez," Gabriel finally said. "Well, José is dead."

"Dead?" Natán quivered.

Gabriel moved his face near to the visitor's. His breath had the air of rotted food.

"Murdered. The victim of wolves disguised as sheep. Those who possess the power of evil could not allow a friend of the Messenger—and I mean a friend, a counselor, a wise man, my right hand—to expose them and save my life. Now you're going to ask why they killed him and left me alive; that is, if you can call this living. No? It doesn't surprise you? Well, I'm going to tell you: because they want to hide their intentions, to turn attention away from themselves, to give another proof of their evil nature, of their intelligence."

As he wiped the iron bedframe with a cloth, he spoke of his presence in the hospital. His family, who loathed him—and the feeling was mutual—had drained its resources in order to reduce him to the humiliating condition of a madman. What was more, the government, which considered him a dangerous individual because he was in possession of secrets that threatened national and global security, was trying to eliminate him.

At moments of his diatribe, Gabriel, agitated to the point of stuttering, paused to grimace before his enemies, to rebuke them in an acerbic tone. Natán tried to keep as still as his chair.

"Good and evil," Gabriel was saying. "You've heard about good and evil? It's all a lie. It's all evil. I'm not going to be taken in by beachheads or bacteria or subterfuges. The founders of religion invented the idea of redemption with a shrewd understanding of human weakness. Politics came along with something more realistic. Vanquishers and victims, rich and poor, heroes and cowards. Each one playing a role as interchangeable as a mask. Wolves disguised as sheep, and vice versa. The Bible, the Koran, Nietzsche, Marx, Jews, Nazis. Fidel Castro shows up as a dirty old redeemer, with a sword as young and fresh as a Cuban palm. Everything is in metaphors. Metaphors are lies. It's a vile world. The Powers are leading us to ruin. The Third World is caught in the trap, and is waiting for its chance to get even. You think the poor and oppressed are better than those who hold the whip? No, sir, they are not. A million times no. The servant is as cruel as the boss. What does he await? A chance to get even. An eye for an eye, a tooth for a tooth. Once upon a time, a hundred years ago, that was my idea. But I got tired of giving in to ideas that turn out to be retreads, no matter how new and exciting they might sound. It's all the same. Nor do I believe any longer in the superman, the man of cultivation and privilege. That's another fallacy. This cell in which they are keeping me a prisoner cannot keep me from having a mind, which runs as free as a river."

"I understand," Natán said in a low voice.

"You cannot possibly understand. But José—he understood. That's why they killed him."

"How?"

"The slaughter of innocents. The evil that goes off on a tangent and harms those who are least implicated, so as to avoid the high court. Love does not exist on this earth. Love is the root of evil. Hatred is its other face, and it turns out the same. I came here to play the role of the indifferent one. That's my mission. Love will not save us. Indifference will. José overstepped the limit. He didn't want to spill blood, so they spilled his. But not as they spilled Christ's! Just the opposite. Christ wanted followers. That was his failing, his sin. I saw José flagellate himself, but not with a conventional whip. Conventionalisms give eternal life to lies. Think about it. My relatives bring me candies and cigarettes. They suffocate me with their love. I am the messenger of indifference. José agreed with me."

"But how did he die? And when?"

Gabriel stretched himself out on the bed and wrapped himself in the sheet.

"Who are you?" he asked, squeezing the sheet against his face until his profile stood out under the white fabric. "Who sent you? The Cuban government or the American? I am, I was a Cuban-American. I went to school in Havana, in New York. I now belong to a higher order, quite beyond this world. Did my family send you to convince me that I should return to the fold and enslave myself?"

"I only want to learn about my brother José," Natán said.

"José had no brothers. Chance was his only life, and that's the greatest expression of indifference. He learned it from me. I myself contributed to his death."

"How?"

A woman's voice, mellifluous and mocking, said from under the sheet: "How? How? Why? Where? When? Questions, little questions, big questions. Stop, Daddy! Daddy! Quit it, Daddy. Stop, Daddy dear."

Natán was on his feet.

"Please excuse me. I didn't mean to bother you. I only wanted to know if you could help me find my brother. I didn't ..."

"You're repeating yourself," Gabriel interrupted in a normal voice. Uncovering his head, he said with hatred: "I'm the one who should be asking how you found me, and who sent you here."

"I told you. José's aunt gave me your phone number. I called and spoke with your family. They told me you were ..."

"Bullshit!" Gabriel exclaimed. "I don't have a family. Nor did José—no brother, no aunts. Now"—he returned to English—*"go back to the little hole you crawled out of."*

"Thank you," Natán said. "This is my card, with my phone number and address. If you would ever like to get in touch with me ..."

"Go to hell!"

Natán hurried away. The wax floor gave a darkened, imprecise reflection of his fleeing form. Patients, doctors and hospital staff, whose faces he avoided, put themselves in his path as if to slow him. The presence of mental illness always made him question his own sanity, as if the line between those realms, already rather vague in his case, threatened to recede and give rise to a common terrain, or perhaps to a tremor, wherein he must resort to a ruse; enter a store and buy something, call the weather bureau and check the readings, lock himself in a bathroom and masturbate, in order to be sure he was normal as far as normalcy went; normal in a world with no room for irrational fears, for self-reproving in front of mirrors, for paranoia or other impudent fantasies.

In the elevator, filled with people whose eyes were fixated by rows of numbers flashing on and off as in a casino—numbers that seemed to determine the course of life—he told and retold himself:

My name is Natán Velázquez. I am a refugee from Cuba. I live in Miami. This is 1991.

He crossed the hospital's lobby, with its furnishings and paintings of cold grandeur, looking askance at the desk where a woman gave assistance to disoriented people as they asked for information of all kinds. On reaching the street, whose unflinching midday light gave no place to hide, he continued to wonder:

Why did I come here? Because I wanted to speak with a friend of my brother's. Why am I sick? Because the man is crazy, and seeing crazy people has made me sick ever since I was a boy. Now I'm going back home. I should wash my clothes. Maybe I'll go to a store and buy a shirt. Long sleeves and a solid color. I don't like the one Sandra gave me, with flowers on it. It's gaudy. Sandra wants me to look younger; as if a fabric with a flower print could change a person's age. I'll get a gray shirt. Or a blue one. Better a shirt with pinstripes, thin ones, they're more elegant. Today is Sunday, January 13.

January 13. The date reminded him of something but he couldn't say what. He got in the car and started to move slowly, paying no mind to the concert of blaring horns that resounded straightaway at his back. Those drivers obviously had good reflexes; but that was natural in a world where speed equaled success and money. He remembered a speaker on English-language TV who had smilingly said, *Life is speed.* At that moment a car whizzed by, and the driver, his face distorted by anger, cried out:

"You son of a bitch!" Natán nodded in agreement. Maybe, he thought, he needed that insult to pull himself together. He sped up a bit. He could turn on the radio; but no, he had had enough of those continuous news bulletins announcing war. A huge billboard was advertising the benefits of some toothpaste; a gigantic smile, with glossy blood-red lips, displayed a set of teeth protruding like sculptures in stone. Another billboard projected a reminder about the fragility of life and the need for an insurance policy to protect your loved ones should you, motorist or pedestrian, become the victim of a sudden death. Ah! Now he remembered. How could he have forgotten? January 13 was the anniversary of his mother's death. It was three years today. Instead of a shirt, he should buy flowers and go to the cemetery.

Submerged at once in the florist's world of outlandish colors—struck dumb by obscene reds of roses, crazed yellows of sunflowers, unsettling violets of orchids, brawny purples of carnations—he chose a branch of pallid lilies, bunched with typical green leaves. His mother had always been fond of flowers, at home and then in exile. Bent over in her garden, she used to complain about the cruelty of ants while she cut the delicate stems of poppies. On both sides of the sea, Natán reflected, flowers and death were one and the same.

Or were they? As he crossed the gleaming lawn of Memorial Gardens, he recalled that in Cuba the burial plots, with their wrought crosses, ornaments and statues, were invested with the solemn attitude of eternity; while in this holy ground of Miami the typical resting place was endowed with a mere tablet, on whose surface you found only the most basic facts of a fleeting existence and a homely epitaph. A cross in relief, tiny and trivial, adorned the upper edge of the stone. A simple vase of flowers—usually artificial, and more durable than the real ones Natán held in his hand—gave a finishing touch to the presumptive resting place.

Nothing here proclaimed the splendor of eternity, the trumpet-calls of the Last Judgment, the delights of heaven, the agonies of hell or the ceaseless wheel of reincarnation; but neither did anything feed the sinister idea that unknown to the naked senses there lived a world of errant, homeless, anguished spirits ready to frighten gullible souls, like Natán himself, who believed that death could produce hideous transfigurations.

It was just a carefully tended garden, crisscrossed by asphalt paths and ringed by a shrub hedge. On the highway beyond, cars went zooming by at racy, riotous speeds.

In the other direction, rows of buildings that looked from afar like warehouses were sheltering the remains of those who had preferred to be kept in vaults, removed from direct contact with the earth. Among these was Natán's mother. A square on an immense wall showed her name and dates. Natán had to stand on tiptoe and stretch his arms in order to place the lilies in the vase of inlaid metal next to the inscription. Then he sat down on a stone bench before the wall, which was entirely covered by plaques and flowers.

Even though it was a Sunday afternoon, the cemetery was quite empty. At moments a car slipped by on the narrow road among the graves, the engine sounding out of place in this region where life was no longer speed. Natán read the names on the wall, most of them Hispanic. At once it occurred to him that if his brother had died, if the story was not another insane invention of Gabriel Perdomo's, then José might be here, too. Destiny, at times, had woven coincidences quite a lot more farfetched. Natán did not have the impulse to go back over the vaults and tombs and look for the name José Velázquez. What, after all, would the name signify? It would signify nothing, as he well knew.

What he felt, quite tangibly, was someone watching him from a hiding place. He had no doubt of it. An unseen stare always gave Natán a pinprick sensation. He got up and looked all around him, even toward the roof, where humidity coming through cracks had made some rough images: faces, animals, mountains. Outside, in the sunlight, among the chatter of invisible birds and the deceptive quiet of tombstones that rose up like miniature islands in a sea of green, someone was watching him. Maybe it was the elderly lady who so carefully washed a stone tablet, as if to wipe away an ignominy. Or maybe it was the downcast young soldier who went crossing by on the gravel pathway.

On the spur of the moment, as if answering a call, Natán spun around. A man in a hat was leaning against a tree with the arrogant self-assurance of someone who keeps watch on a territory and doesn't like a stranger showing up. His look made Natán shudder. He gave back an obligatory gesture of greeting, an imprecise motion of his hand. Then the unknown man turned his head, lowered his hat and hurried away.

The fellow didn't weave around the tombstones but in his surprising flight—his rapid step couldn't be anything else—he walked over the stones, he almost jumped from one to another; and, as it had rained at noon, his shoes were treading mud on the names of the dead. He even kicked over a vase of flowers. A part of Natán wanted to run after him—the man had a familiar face he couldn't make out—but he was frozen with amazement. While eyeing the figure that moved away with increasing speed, Natán turned back to the bench facing the vault where his mother had been at rest for three years.

"I should fix those lilies," he told himself, passing a hand through his hair. The other man was now leaving the cemetery by the main gate, and didn't look back.

Natán, who had accepted his mother's death without despair—who within a few short weeks after the funeral had gone for days and, more lately, months without thinking of her—now felt an overpowering desire to have her at his side, even though their relationship had never expressed itself in physical affection, in hugs or kisses, which mother and son alike had shunned.

"I'm regressing, this is a momentary weakness, nothing of consequence," he said out loud, then looked around to make sure no one was listening.

No one was.

Maybe that was the reason for his anguish: no one listening. These last years he had isolated himself, had stopped visiting his childhood friends who like himself had taken the path of exile, and his relations had become formalized, courteous to extremes, because Natán, while being a genuinely amiable person, could not show warmth or intimacy.

He pursued companionship by sexual means alone; but each time he wound up tiring of the "momentary" woman, as he was now tired of Sandra, and with each passing affair the void grew deeper. Teresa, his married neighbor, was the first to have awakened in Natán a feeling like love; but Natán knew he could only count on her for chance occasions—thirty minutes of wordless passion that merely made him sadder—and then his skin rejected those humid, spotted bed-sheets, which ended in a heap at the bottom of his laundry.

Now, in a setting that evoked the endpoint of everything human—or perhaps its transmutation into something unknown and, for that very reason, macabre—he would have wanted to hold Teresa in his arms, kiss her armpits, put his head on her breasts; but his lover was nowhere near, and he couldn't even arrange an appointment with her.

He went out of the cemetery and drove around aimlessly. The street-lamps and neon signs were gradually lighting up. From some restaurants came an odor of food, murmuring voices, music and laughter. A sign for a naked ladies' show projected playful images in the gathering darkness.

In the murkiness of the ladies' bar, which reeked of smoke and vibrated with the harmonies of an Eric Clapton song, Natán felt instantly at ease—especially when a young woman with an overweening bust, nipples hard and pointed, took him to a table near the stage, also managing to graze his arm with her breasts.

"A beer," Natán said in a stammer as he sat down. "No, whisky is better."

"Whisky is always better," the girl agreed with a knowing smile. Those exposed breasts reinforced her words and gestures—amplified them. Yes, Natán told himself, those were amplifier breasts. Even more, they wiped away the anguish of loneliness, madness and death; of green lawns dappled with tombstones, of strangers that lean on trees and spy on you and run away.

"Thanks," Natán said. "You don't know how good you've made me feel."

"I can dance for you, right here, next to your lap. It costs ten dollars a dance."

Natán thought of how much money he had on him. He had plenty, but he wanted to use it for drinks.

"No thanks, just bring me the whisky and I'll watch the show."

Yes, he thought afterward, this was the better choice. A dancer on stage, lit up by spastic reflectors, maneuvered with remarkable skill. Covered by no more than a strip around her thigh where mountains of crumpled bill-notes were compressed, she was much more attractive than the waitress. Her elastic body stretched and folded; her hands probed the furry regions of her beautiful figure; her limbs gyrated to the music with bold energy—but what held him in thrall, as he relished his drink, was her bush in the shape of a heart. The hairs had been shaved to replicate that shape exactly: a heart of pubis, dark and quivering, moistened by a delicate sweat. As plush as a cushion, and maybe as soft. Natán would have wanted to recline his head on that pillow, to feel the gentle circulation of blood, to forget his arid life. A cushion of grass next to a spring where he could wash away his anxiety. Surely that would cost too much. If the other girl wanted ten dollars to dance for him, this one would ask a hundred to admit him to that heart of hair. And it wouldn't avail to haggle over the price. He might as well resign himself to another whisky, and to the comforts of the dark.

At dawn he awoke in an unfamiliar room, with the word 'NO' written in huge, crooked strokes on the ceiling exactly above his head. It was a small, foul-smelling room with a bed, table and chair. A glare of streetlights poured in through the open window, suffusing the room with a sallow tinge. The roar of a siren sounded in the distance. Natán got up with difficulty, his muscles and skull aching, and leaned out the window. His mouth was extremely dry and tasted dreadful. On the sidewalk of a deserted street, two black women dressed to the nines were insulting each other pitilessly. Even if his English was nearly perfect, all Natán could make out was the word 'fucking,' which bounded between them with utmost energy in the thickened silence of night. Naked, he sat down on the edge of the bed. He tried to remember how he had gotten to this place. He saw himself in the girlie bar, putting dollar bills in the dancer's thigh, under the sash, very near the design. He kissed her on the foot; her painted toenails were shining like mother-of-pearl. He remembered a large mole on her knee.

Stumbling out of bed, still tipsy, he found the small bathroom. When he caught sight of himself in the mirror, the reflection of his bloated face gave him another clue to the night before. A fleeting image: he was leaving the bar with someone, a woman; not the dancer or even the waitress but another lady with Indian features, who didn't stop talking in a strong Central American accent. A man was following them at a distance, at moments touching the brim of his hat. Natán had turned on him and, hurling insults, challenged him to fight. The other guy, without answering, crossed to the other sidewalk and kept going in the same direction, pausing before a window display. Natán believed it was the same man who had been spying on him at the cemetery.

"Chicken! Queer!" Natán had shouted.

The woman was pulling him along, begging him not to get into a fix. They went back to the bar's parking lot to get Natán's car. The man, it seemed, had gone into a store. Natán and the woman drove to this hotel, doubtless chosen by her. He had taken her, or maybe he hadn't. He only had a vague image of heady embraces in the darkness, of whispered obscenities—and once more he was enveloped in an alcoholic mist.

He splashed water on his face and hair, all the while telling himself he must not repeat this absurd adventure. Even if he enjoyed drinking and going on binges, he was not a lush or a whoremonger. He picked up his wrinkled shirt, which seemed to him ridiculously small, not nearly his size; then his pants and underclothes, which hung in the bathroom accusingly, and started to dress. His wallet, of course, was empty.

He crept out of the sordid hotel. In the center of the sky a lunatic moon was still shining, while dawn's uncertain clarity could be seen just beyond the empty streets. As he drove across Miami's northern suburbs, he listened to radio reports about the coming war. It was now a question of hours; thousands of soldiers on both sides could soon be dead.

Natán would have liked to feel himself moved by the imminence of tragedy; but thoughts of fields darkened by smoke and blood, of bombers dispersing destruction, of unknown corpses covered with desert sand, failed to rouse any part of him—not even his dread of death. All he wanted was to sleep. When he reached his apartment, daylight had fully emerged.

FIVE

Besieged by a toxic hangover, Natán stayed in bed for two days, only getting up to go to the bathroom and kitchen—plunged in lethargy, suffering from nausea, nightmares and fearfulness, as confined as a castaway on a deserted isle, only without the sensory stimuli of sea, sky and vegetation. His only relief came from his neighbor and lover, who twice a day brought him a piping hot soup or a fruit milkshake. She also lay down beside him—not to make love, since the illness had stopped up that drive, but to speak in a whisper about her daughters' mischief or the bitterness of life with her husband, to whom she felt tied by law, duties, obligations, vows, but never by affection or affinity. She recounted her childhood in Cuba, on the outskirts of Havana, under the sway of a neurotic mother, a widow and religious cultist; and she told of her adolescence on the outskirts of Madrid—she had never lived entirely in the country or in the city, which might explain why she was not at home anywhere—brought up by a Galician aunt and uncle who lived in a past of wealth and glory that the land of Castille had absorbed as desert sands consume a rainstorm.

Natán listened with eyes closed, at times losing the thread of her story but grateful for her voice, her accent, her fragrance, her companionship, and he thought that never before—not even in the cusp of their lovemaking, which always unfolded in silence—had he felt so close to Teresa as in those two days.

When she disappeared, his frustration and anxiety started again. He kept getting up to drink water and go to the toilet—making sure to avoid the obdurate mirror—then went back to bed, where a blank ceiling and a horde of inhospitable memories were waiting for him.

Natán hadn't wanted to tell Teresa about the excesses of that Sunday, or about the fruitless, ongoing search for his brother, or especially about the advent of a stranger or apparition who might be trying to extract something from him. All he knew was that in looking for his father's son he had called forth a hostile presence from which he could not free himself. Who else was the fisherman—to give him some kind of name—planted since dawn Monday on the lakeshore opposite? Natán had paid him no heed when, back home from the hotel, he had gone out on his balcony, still quite drunk, to breathe the morning air. In the afternoon, after a brief visit from Teresa, whom he'd ventured to call and tell he was sick, and as he drank her soup near his glass door while watching the eccentric flight of water-birds, he still had not felt surprise on seeing the same man, or another much like him, in the same spot. A patient, stubborn fisherman, he had thought—but in the wee hours, when after being visited by nightmares he had again gone out on his balcony for some solace in the serenity of the landscape and found the same figure hunched over the dark water, looking rather like a shrub that had been whimsically parted from the vegetation in the forest behind, Natán understood the figure was there in specific relation to himself.

Today, Wednesday, back at work, he pushed himself to organize the mounds of papers on his desk that kept threatening to topple over. The boss came and went with a disgruntled look. Every time the phone rang, Natán felt his stomach contract as if the device were part of his innards. After four hours of feigning concentration and playing the businessman with a veteran actor's technique, he went out for lunch.

His habit nowadays was to go to a little Cuban cafeteria on the corner whose owner, an aging lady with a motherly bosom, greeted her regular clients with nicknames. "Here comes the dog!" she blurted, or "Here comes Captain Spider!" or "Miss Universe!" or "The Frogman!" Natán—he himself knew not why—was "The Dreamer."

No one resisted these labels. Natán liked the place for its cheap and tasty food—and despite the grime and grease-spots turning up surreptitiously on the counter, walls, plates and utensils, he enjoyed those minutes of pretending to be part of a country he had long ago left; part of a people who shared a distinctive speech, a careless sincerity, an easy smile, an irascible temper, an impudent charm; and as the fragrant vapor of black beans clouded his eyes, as he took in the chatter of his fellow diners, he somehow made contact with that remnant of himself.

He couldn't avoid the truth. Between himself and that country where he had experienced fleeting moments of happiness amid long periods of misfortune, the tie had grown frayed, perhaps beyond repair. The idea of "the fatherland," a mental cornerstone on which many of his fellow countrymen in America had built their lives, had lost meaning for Natán. Surely, if the government in Cuba were to change, he might think of going back, but not in answer to a higher call. If he went, it would be to get away from that lake in front of his balcony, from the reflection of those trees in the water, from the highways where life equaled speed, from those voices on the phone, from insomnia—from himself.

The idealism of his youth—his desire to rage against the big lie that was devouring, piece by piece, the country he called "fatherland"—had dissolved in impotence and yielded to a chronic skepticism. Cubans, on the island as well as in exile, were tearing each other apart with words and deeds. Laziness, jealousy, lust for power, ill will and a pervasive spying on one's fellows had wiped out any chance for a recovery.

Even so, he kept up his daily visits to that cafeteria teeming with people who, between word-plays, political harangues and gossip, feasted on tongue-scalding soups, mountains of rice, fatty meats and sauces. He felt joy as well as compassion whenever he heard news of refugees who, in growing numbers, managed to reach these shores on rafts, boats or hijacked planes.

Today, however, Natán could hardly bear the jokes, rumors and slander that seasoned the heavy food. He was also irritated by noise from ventilators in the ceiling. He left his shrimp in cocktail sauce half uneaten, paid without leaving a tip and went out.

"First comes the feed, then comes the dream," the old lady said when she saw him go. Natán didn't tell her what he thought: no one can have dreams in a dive like this.

Back at the office he tried to get Alicia Lastre on the phone, but her line was insistently busy. He supposed José's aunt must be tied up in some extended talk with a friend her age, swapping stories about ailments, symptoms, medications, family deaths, daily tragedies; but after three hours of trying, he figured the phone must be off the hook or out of order. At the end of his workday he decided to visit her.

As he knocked at the door of her apartment in Little Havana, where a cat rubbing itself against the staircase eyed him with apprehension, he wondered whether he should tell the old lady that someone had been pursuing him since his last visit. "Pursuing," he told himself, was too dramatic. Perhaps he need only describe the appearances of the stranger or strangers—as he couldn't be sure he was dealing with just one person—and tell her he felt these visits were mysteriously related to his search for José. He imagined Alicia Lastre would not show any great surprise; a long life plus a premonition of death would make her understanding and accepting.

He knocked four times without getting an answer. He tried turning the handle and gave a start when the door just opened.

"Alicia," he said softly, then more loudly and with a quiver: "Alicia!"

He went into the sitting room with its motley collection of furniture and knickknacks. The old lady's favorite chair, which had been with her through all her years of exile, bore the imprint of her body, as if she had just risen out of it. In the corner, on the altar, a pair of snub-nosed candles, almost liquefied, cast a flickering light on a small statue of the Virgin and a faded bouquet of roses. The strange brightness that Natán had found so disturbing on his prior visit was gone; in its place was a quiet semidarkness. Now he could see that the ceiling was perfectly flat, with no skylight, only marked by the thinnest of cobwebs.

The place exuded camphor, humidity, cologne. Indistinct voices from elsewhere in the building magnified the silence. The decorative porcelain, exquisitely personal, seemed to cry out against Natán's intrusion.

"Alicia," he said again, without conviction.

He put the phone handle back on its cradle; it had not been

correctly replaced. In the kitchen he was struck by the glistening of crystalware and cutlery. He would never have thought to eat or drink from such things; they looked like objects for use in a religious ceremony. He drew back the curtain that separated the apartment from a small balcony and the building's interior court— a squalid, empty square. He threw a glance into the spotless bathroom. Then, with trepidation, he opened the door to the bedroom. He saw no bed, no furniture, nothing that would suggest an occupant, only magazine pages on the floor. The closet was likewise empty but for two prayer books.

Natán leafed through them and found a photo of Alicia sitting in her chair, looking with pleasure back at the lens. Behind her, leaning against a wall, was the face of his own father, just as he had remembered it from thirty years before, with lips distended into a faint smile. Natán's heart gave a leap at the sight of that face. Only after a few moments did he realize that this young man with hair gone completely white, discreetly elegant in dress, a reflexive expression giving his features an abstracted feel, must be his half-brother José.

Alicia must have forgotten she had this photo—although, judging from her appearance, it was quite recent. Who could have taken it? Mercedes and Gladys had both told him they never visited José's aunt. It might have been Gabriel Perdomo, just prior to the illness that deprived him of his sanity. Maybe it was a neighbor or a distant relative. Maybe it was an automatic camera, strategically deployed to fix the old lady and her nephew for a fleeting instant before José resumed his traveling life.

So he was real. Natán grasped that until now he had doubted José's existence, as if the man's many traces had not been enough to convince him. He *did* have a brother. There he was, the man, his brother—his brother. The kinship was undeniable. Indeed, José was much more like their father than Natán, whose face took after his mother's.

Hearing footsteps outside, he pocketed the photo and stepped into the hallway. An elderly couple, arm in arm, had started down the staircase.

"Excuse me," Natán said, approaching them. "I'm a friend of Alicia Lastre's, I came to see her, the door was open but ..."

"Alicia died last week. It was quite sudden," the man said, adjusting his eyeglasses as if to see a document up close. Indeed, he was reading Natán.

"A heart attack," the lady explained. "And who would you be?"

"A friend of the family."

"Family?" the woman said. "In that case, let me tell you that if Alicia had family, they treated her very poorly. We had no way of reaching anybody. *Anybody.*"

"She had a nephew," Natán said.

"No nephew, nobody," the lady said pointedly. "The only ones at the funeral were her neighbors—and as we used to say in Cuba, it was stinking poor. That's what happens when you get old and you're far away from your country, and you haven't been able to save any money. People become heartless over here."

"I'm so sorry," Natán said, as if he were to blame.

The lady's withered face came alive as she raised her accusing tone.

"Sure, now we get the grief, the pangs of conscience, when it's too late! You have no idea what it means to come to the end of your life completely abandoned, completely alone, far from your native land, your fatherland...."

"That's true, the fatherland," Natán murmured and bowed his head.

"Go ahead and make jokes," the lady kept dogging him. "Some day ..."

56

"*Señora*, how can you think I'm making jokes ..."

"This gentleman isn't joking, Lucía," her husband broke in, gently tugging her along. "Please excuse her, she's out of herself with grief."

"I am *not* out of myself! I am only telling the truth! And no one should dare touch a thing in that apartment! Alicia willed it all to the Salvation Army, she gave that instruction many times, it's what she wanted, but people have been going in and taking her things. How irresponsible, to leave the door open! I'm going to talk to the building manager this minute. People can just go and steal what they want. Woe unto anyone who takes a thing! And if the shoe fits, wear it."

Natán put on a smile. "*Señora*, I don't need anything in there. I have a good job and a good salary."

The woman moved her aged body like a wild animal on the hunt.

"A good job and a good salary! Listen to that! Did you hear, Fernando? Alicia had a pension that couldn't buy her anything! She had to come to us for money because nobody was there to help! Her family never showed up, she was a lonely old lady, lonely in her soul, and now you have the nerve to come here and say you have a good job and a good salary!"

"But I was not a relative!"

"Family or friend, what's the difference!"

"Let's go, Lucía, don't fret yourself! Come along, my love. Remember what the doctor said."

Natán retreated to the apartment, drenched in sweat.

"If you take a thing, I'll turn you in to the police!" the old lady screamed at him from the stairway.

The stale air in the room made breathing almost impossible. Sitting on the sofa near the altar, catching sight of his own agitated face in a cloudy mirror, Natán waited a few minutes to make sure the couple was gone and stole out of the place like a criminal, feeling the photo in his shirt pocket.

Back at his place he drew the curtain across his sliding-glass door without so much as a glance at the lake; he didn't want to know whether the mysterious figure on the opposite shore was present or absent. He was disquieted to note that either possibility frightened him. With all his suspicion and aversion, a solid bond had been forged between the stranger and himself.

That night, for the third time, he sat down to answer his father's letter. The words went helter-skelter on the page, exuding resentment and confusion; the letters got smaller, then bigger, then spread all over until the pages were stained with ink. He was quite ready to leave off this filial task, now postponed for two months, when Sandra showed up in a nervous excitement.

"They're bombing Baghdad! Turn on the TV!" she exclaimed as she came in. Her outfit was a gaudy jacket-and-pants affair. She was enveloped in a cloud of fragrance and impeccably made up.

"What for? I'm writing my father."

"I tell you, they're bombing Baghdad! Don't you get it? This is war! War!" And taking up the remote control, she turned on the TV.

Natán, who strove to please his lover in all matters except that of living together, grabbed the gadget away from her and turned off the TV.

"I'm sorry, Sandra, but this war is none of my business. Baghdad is on the other side of the world. Besides, I don't go in for news."

"You're off your rocker," Sandra said, baffled. "Do you have another woman here?"

Stamping her heels, she made for the bedroom, opened the closet doors, looked under the bed, went into the bathroom and pulled aside the shower curtain. Natán followed her in silence and anger.

"You're the one who's off your rocker," he said finally. "What the hell is the point of this mistrust? It's ridiculous, just ridiculous."

Sandra reinspected every nook and cranny. Her throat was quivering, and her complexion shone red even under the makeup. She headed for the balcony.

"Go there if you want, but leave the curtain alone," Natán said. "The light bothers me."

"What light, you imbecile? Don't you see it's night?"

"The night lights bother me."

"No! I'm the one who bothers you."

"You've got a point," Natán said, and instantly regretted saying it as he saw this woman on whom he had foisted himself hardly a year ago, and from whom he now sought escape, run to the balcony in tears.

Natán followed her and put his hand on her shoulder, with the same sort of cursory kindness you show to a stranger who's been struck by a sudden tragedy. Then he caressed her hair, lately dyed, also looking out at the dark surface of the lake and the trees on the other shore, where he found no human figure. A hapless breeze made waves on the waters, jostled the boats at the dock and swayed the tops of the pines. A perfectly round and sallow moon jutted above the distant Miami skyscrapers like an enormous, useless lamp.

"Sandra, please excuse me. I've got some difficulties in my life— I'm dealing with a ton of things."

"What things?"

"Private things. I can't mention them. It's kind of a crisis. I need some time."

Sandra fixed her hair.

"Your only crisis is that you don't love me—not me, not anybody or anything. You don't even care about your country."

"Which country?"

"What do you mean, which country? *This* country, obviously—the one that opened its doors to you, the one that made you feel like a human being after those people in Cuba crushed you like a cockroach—or so you told me when we met. Have you forgotten? And now that this country gets into a war whose ending no one knows, you tell me it's none of your business, and Baghdad is far away, or whatever."

"Sandra, it's not so simple. Of course I'm grateful to this country, but I have nothing to do with politics or war or anything of the kind. How do I pay my debt to society? By watching people die on a TV screen in my living room? That's not gratitude, it's morbid curiosity."

"Okay, that's true, but something else is going on. I know what I'm talking about. It's a coldness, a monstrous indifference. You're a man with no feelings."

"I wish I were."

"With me you are."

"I think I've shown you otherwise."

"I'm not talking about sex. I mean caring—acting like a human being."

"I *am* a human being—human, all too human. Nietzsche wrote a book by that name ..."

"Stop! You see what I mean? For you, life is just a big joke. You turn everything to shit."

"That might be true. This afternoon a lady who doesn't know me said something like that. Or maybe I don't show who I really am."

Natán went back to the living room and turned on the TV set. A map of the Middle East filled up the screen. A reporter's voice, distorted by a telephone line, was describing an attack on the Iraqi capital: a tremendous roar of planes, columns of black smoke shooting up in the night, masses of people in terror. Several times Natán changed the channel, but they were all showing the same things: interviews with military experts or officials or leaders of groups whose initials Natán didn't recognize; anxious relatives of soldiers who had gone to Saudi Arabia; and reporters who were visibly enjoying their moments of fame.

Sandra quietly sat down next to him.

Natán knew all too well the ominous distance that arises between two people who are about to break it off. He clearly recognized the lack of tender phrases, the sense of erosion and emptiness, the recoiling from physical contact. As he watched images reaching his home from faraway places that he would surely never visit, he was distressed by the closeness of this woman who had tried to rally her fading beauty in an effort to reconquer him. He wanted to take pity on her, but all he could feel was the frustration of someone who has made the same old mistake one more time and knows he has to face the music. After an hour of impudent silence he said:

"Sandra, I'm not good enough for you."

The woman got to her feet like a puppet pulled by wires and paced about the room with tears in her eyes.

"I don't want to begin all over again," she finally said. "But I can see you've already decided."

"I haven't decided anything—but I can't give you what you're looking for, what you need. I'm sorry, but that's the way it is."

"I don't think you're sorry at all."

"Think what you will."

Just then Sandra noticed, on the telephone table, the photo Natán had brought with him earlier in the evening.

"Who is that old woman?" she said sourly.

"It's my half-brother's aunt. And he's the man in back of her. He's just like my father."

"That must be another photo. In this one she's by herself."

"By herself?" The question came out like a scream.

"What's the matter with you?"

"Let me see that," he said, reaching out and trying to control his sudden shaking.

Alicia Lastre was in her chair, leaning on the headrest, smiling peacefully, surrounded by her porcelain miniatures. In a corner was a piece of the altar, and nearby a pair of landscapes decorating the wall. All traces of another human presence had vanished.

"You're right." Natán had gone hoarse. "I guess she forgot to give me the other photo."

"When did you see her?"

"When? Today or yesterday—I think it was yesterday."

"And what does she say?"

"Who, Alicia? Nothing—nothing special. You know old people, they just complain about their illnesses."

Sandra drew a breath. On the TV, some youngsters were demonstrating in front of the White House, shouting peace slogans, rebounding with youthful energy and quite aware of the camera's all-seeing lens.

"You can turn that off if you want to, you don't have to keep it on for my sake."

Natán had not taken his eyes away from that colorful rectangle where multitudes were yelling.

"It doesn't bother me."

"It *was* bothering you."

"Now it's not."

"I think I'll go."

"Very well, Sandra."

"I'm not coming back. I'm fed up."

"I understand."

She went out, slamming the door. The blow shook the walls and windows but hardly registered with Natán, who calmly stayed before the rapid succession of images. Then, slowly, he pulled open the curtain.

Beyond the glass door, the full moon, which had come to the center of the sky, brilliantly lit the lake. Natán went out on the balcony. Leaves and branches rustled in the breeze. On the shore near the forest, beside the uneasy water, someone was walking aimlessly.

"What do you want from me?" Natán said in a low voice. "If it's you, come over here and talk to me. At least give me a sign."

The figure kept up its erratic route, coming and going, at times motionless like someone waiting, at others moving in circles like someone scouting new territory or simply enjoying the cool night air, then disappeared into the pines.

How can you find out if a person you're trying to locate is dead?

The question came to Natán when he woke up after a night crowded with dreams that a strong sedative had given him; and it stayed with him all day long.

When Natán told his boss he suspected a relative had died and he had no way of confirming it, the boss—an extremely practical man, except in his abnormal weakness for women, on whom he wasted fortunes—advised him to go to a Social Security office, or make a Missing Persons report, or, failing all else, hire a private investigator.

"But don't ask for much," the boss added. "Detectives cost real money."

"I'm doing this for my father, who's quite sick in Cuba. He's asked me to find my half-brother."

"Then start with Social Security."

"Actually I was thinking I might take a trip. Someone told me he might be in New York," Natán said. He was surprised at how easily impromptu lies took shape on his lips. "I think I have some vacation time coming, don't I? I haven't gone anywhere for more than a year; and I believe they abolished slavery some time ago."

"Fine, then, two weeks, but no more. In March they begin repairing the boats in Cumaná and I need you there alert, eyes open, not the way you've been lately. You seem to be in another world. What the hell's going on, anyway? Have you fallen in love?"

"Maybe."

"Whatever you do, don't marry! I've got five divorces under my belt and another on the way. Women are not a blessing."

"When can I take off?"

"Today, if you feel like it. It's dead around here; but first close the deal with that son of a bitch in Maracaibo who wants to buy the engine. Don't go for more than two weeks, okay? I want you to come back refreshed, we ought to make real money this year. This war is a boon to Venezuela; oil prices are going through the roof. We'll be swimming in a sea of cash."

At his house Natán made straight for the balcony, like someone hurrying to check the damage a fire has done to his house. The lake and forest were quite deserted. He had a presentiment and snatched up the photo of Alicia. His intuition had not betrayed him. Behind the old lady, leaning on a wall, he again found the man who looked so like his father, wearing a white shirt, a tie, and a pensive expression that seemed to take in the changing world of posterity—the long and perhaps endless line of people who would hold this picture in their hands for years to come. Natán felt the impulse to burn the photo or tear it to pieces; but then he realized he would not thereby break his bond with the stranger.

Nor was he inclined to pursue the strictly logical routes his boss had suggested—to tie himself up in bureaucratic traps and searches that at most could give him bare facts like the ones Alicia and the ex-girlfriends and even Gabriel Perdomo, from inside his delirium, had offered. With a bit of luck, he might be able to confirm that José Velázquez was actually dead; but such discoveries would not provide what he most wanted, which was a means of communication. That, or so he told himself, was the goal toward which he was working: to communicate; to extend a bridge across darkness toward his brother. That was it. Facts were beside the point, and the photo, like all photos, was a piece of cardboard, shiny and voiceless.

In days following, Natán felt, as he had not in years, the strength of purpose one derives from having a goal. At times his ignorance was a shock to him, as if he had reached an unknown land where people spoke a language he barely understood. He had to follow customs foreign to his own; to deal with people who had no relation to him and treated him with open hostility.

Lacking a map, or an instruction manual, or a friendly hand that could show him the way, he set himself to scour the streets of Miami—looking at commercial signs, at the faces of infrequent pedestrians, and at houses ringed with iron bars that showed the same warnings: *Beware of Dog. No Soliciting. Keep Your Distance. Do Not Enter.* He opened the newspaper for a helpful piece of news, a word to guide him, even a coded message. He listened to songs of love or despair on the radio, trying to find a clue or uncover a conspiracy.

Meanwhile, throughout the city, flags had sprung up everywhere—flags of all sizes, in shop windows, on auto antennas, telephone poles, roofs, trees and balconies; and also yellow ribbons that expressed faith in the victorious return of soldiers now fighting in far-off, unimaginable places. Radio announcers, in English and Spanish, called on people to show solidarity with allied armies that battled against the Iraqi invaders of Kuwait.

Natán, who was not insensitive to ideas of justice, liberty or heroism, would have wished to feel inspired by this display of patriotic fervor; but he was ashamed to recognize that in his present situation, such thoughts would only distract him from his goals.

Parallel to this collective fervor, which Cubans in Miami had embraced with the natural yearning of exiled people who dream about the liberation of their homeland, Natán discovered a hidden, underground life that bore no relation to the rampant materialism of the city and rather contradicted it: a flowering of sects, astrologers, spiritual advisors, fortune tellers; the disquieting presence of small shops, or *botánicas,* that sold statues of the Virgin to banish misfortunes, potions to subdue unfaithful lovers, prayers to produce money, herbs to cure illnesses that science couldn't remedy, perfumes to dispel curses, protective collars, sea-shells that announced future events, even animals for making sacrifices to exigent gods. Conferences about the occult, black magic and theosophy proliferated. Natán saw larger-than-life statues of saints appearing in the gardens of handsome residences; and he noticed how many more vehicles were trying to crowd into church parking lots on Saturdays and Sundays.

Perhaps, he thought, these signs of a faith that rejected all reason had long abounded in Miami, but up to now he had never noticed them.

His childhood and teenage years had progressed under two opposite influences: the political fanaticism of his father, who as a Communist Party official and "revolutionary" standard-bearer had scorned any display of religious feeling; and the religious fanaticism of his mother, an old-fashioned Catholic whose devout and infertile life had stagnated to the point of denying the outside world. When at last the hoped-for divorce had taken place, Natán— an only child, or so he believed, and as unhappy with his father's ideology as he was with his mother's beliefs—had stubbornly tried to create his own personal system of values. After lengthy struggles replete with failure and backward movement, he had become what he was today: a man with no moorings, too sensitive to be a skeptic and too distrustful to believe in anything. The phrases from that hymn he had so often heard in Cuba, sung by ardent masses—*Away with all your superstitions/ No more deluded by reaction/ No saviour from on high delivers/ No faith have we in prince or peer*—he applied to the political system under which he now lived, just as he would apply it to any other.

When he joined the exiles, the drive to enrichment he saw in his fellows aroused his disdain. In time, his own industry won him a big salary and comfortable lifestyle; but material well-being, as he had always suspected and could now affirm, was not a solid foundation in life. So at this awkward moment, when he considered himself the victim of events that he must against his grain call supernatural—and as he was determined at all costs to unravel the mystery—he felt some relief at finding he was not alone in calling on recondite powers.

During the weekend he visited several clairvoyants. He began with an American lady astrologer who entered the date, hour and place of his birth in her computer. Fifteen minutes later she gave him a copy of his birth chart. The symbols of bygone epochs, especially of the dark Middle Ages, looked spotlessly modern in the faultless design of the printout, which nonetheless took away some of the *gravitas* he was expecting from such a coded record of his past and future. The reading contained information one could have gathered from a cursory acquaintance with him. An Aquarius with an ascendant in Gemini—the lady explained with unsteady hands and tired eyes—Natán's life had unfolded largely in the realms of his mind. The difficult place for him, she added, was home and family. Those relationships were a constant source of disquiet.

Natán, who had been incredulous until the astrologer said that, showed some interest.

"That's why I came here," he said.

"I'm seeing frustration and discord here," the lady said as her fingernail, a strident purple, pointed to symbols recalling the Greek alphabet. "A tension between mismatched personalities. Your rational faculties block out the emotional currents that flow to you from others. Of course it's not so simple. With the stars, as in life, nothing is simple."

"That's for sure," Natán said with a sigh.

"This conjunction of Saturn and the sun reflects a period of crisis. The moon is also being disturbed by Saturn and, to boot," she added with some distress, "Mars is taking an aspect from Pluto, which could be a sign of violence in the future. The influence of Mars on Pluto could even signify danger to your life."

Natán swallowed.

"I don't see the reason for that," he said.

"Here we have another meaningful sign," the woman said. "Do you see this conjunction? This is the fourth house, the house of family. Neptune is in transit here."

The lady astrologer kept up her talk, teeming with obscure terminology which Natán forced himself to follow attentively, motionless in his chair, shivering slightly in the strong currents of air-conditioning that swept across the office, where tapestries of celestial maps hung on the wall. He was fascinated by the woman's wrinkles and by the circles under her eyes, which appeared to deepen as she spoke. After a good while, getting the sense that this lavish expenditure of phrases, which became more abstract with every turn, was not going to give him any real help, Natán interrupted brusquely.

"I think this is enough. I'm expected somewhere for lunch and

I'm already quite late. Thank you very much. What do I owe?"

Outside, in the tiny vestibule, which had been empty when Natán had arrived, four women and a man were waiting. Despite the differences in age and facial features, they looked rather alike, though at that moment he couldn't say how. In sessions to come, the same ambiguous faces would reappear in search of a word of solace or warning—a shield against misfortune, a straight line through their confused and tortured lives.

In other such offices, while he waited his turn, he watched fellow customers as they swapped stories in low voices: wives with drunken or philandering husbands, mothers with drug-addicted children, men besieged with sudden illnesses or secret vices, teenagers on the brink of suicide, widows who couldn't accept the loss of their life partners, spinsters keeping up a vestige of hope, young victims of abuse, people whose loved ones had betrayed them.

"Those faces ..." Natán thought—and he didn't find a way to end the sentence. Then he told himself: Something sets those faces apart from others. And on leaving, having heard whatever message the stars or the cards or the runic stones or the sea-shells or the lines of one's own hand had had to tell in their enigmatic way, he looked in the rearview mirror to see if his own face might be showing the telltale sign that, with the passage of days, he had come to call *the face of loneliness.*

Yes, he thought, his face was like those others. He was driving under Miami's unrelenting sun, which burned even in midwinter. Dazzled by the naked light, bewildered by clouds of steam that hovered above burning asphalt, he kept scanning those clips of newspaper ads with addresses of people who announced themselves as present-day oracles—a pursuit for which he had budgeted five hundred dollars, not because he actually believed in this business, for up to now the answers he had gotten were vague or contradictory, with no one able to pinpoint the object of his search, but rather because he wanted to exhaust all possibilities.

Not since the night of his break-up with Sandra had he seen the elusive figure. He still had that photo of Alicia and José in his shirt pocket, and in his wallet he carried the handwritten poem he had found in the guard-shack at Miami Lakes. While he couldn't say that those verses had anything to do with his half-brother, neither would he discard the idea.

That poem led him to look up a friend of his youth, a fellow student at Havana University, from which both had been expelled for "political problems" before they could finish their courses of study, Natán's being sociology, Antonio's mathematics. His old buddy, a scholar who had not taken well to life in exile, worked at a library and scarcely left his house in Perrine, where he lived with his wife, a teacher of literature. Their son had perished in an accident three years before. After the tragedy, Natán had gone to see him several times and then had limited himself to an occasional phone call. Antonio was a highly sensitive man who did not hide his feelings. One had only to speak the word "Cuba" for his face to redden and his breath to grow heavy, like an asthmatic's. Whenever they spoke, Natán avoided all mention of the past—an omission that had made their talks difficult.

Now, after they had exchanged some trifles on the phone, Natán accepted an invitation to join them for a meal. Antonio also said: "Afterward we're going to a lecture about Teilhard de Chardin. A lady we know is giving the talk. Why don't you come with us?"

Natán found it an extremely positive sign. The fact that his friends were going out to an event—and one about a thinker who had tried to reconcile science and faith—meant that they, too, had embarked on a search.

No sooner had he crossed their threshold and given the customary *abrazos,* his hosts brightening at the sight of their visitor, than Natán felt a weight on his chest. The photos of their boy, who had died at just nineteen, and whose growing-up Natán had seen, covered the walls, bookcases, tables and piano. The pictures showed him at every stage of his life, from his infancy in Cuba up to the last days of his youth, in high-school graduation garb at a Miami academy, or in a shiny new sports car in front of a Fort Lauderdale gym. Natán couldn't forget the photo in his shirt pocket—at this moment he was sure José, too, had died—and he shrank away from the sight of that child, that boy, that youth full of smiles forever trapped in picture frames, forced into an eternal show of happiness.

Against Natán's expectations, Antonio and Gloria sounded content. They filled up the gaps of conversation with questions, even with good-natured jokes about Natán and his reluctance to marry.

During the meal they spoke of friends in common, noting once more their surprise at the different paths they had all taken, whether they had left their country or stayed there. Long-forgotten names and faces hovered intrepidly above the roast; the men traded happy anecdotes from their student days while Gloria skillfully sliced the loin-meat or plucked bad leaves out of the salad.

"I see you don't get so worked up nowadays when you talk about Cuba," Natán said with gentle irony, spurred on by wine that had loosened his tongue.

"My son's death," Antonio said, looking nervously at his wife and quickly correcting himself, "our son's death has taught me to see things in a different light. It gave me some distance, a way of looking through a prism. I can't really explain. It's a kind of consciousness, an absence of motion—well, that's not it, either. It's the same melody but played in a different tempo. I know it sounds ridiculous. Not only do you understand that everything you love or hate is relative; but even more, the passions, and of course I mean the useless passions, have been cleansed away."

"I understand," Natán said. "I'm full of useless passions."

Slowly he cast his eye over the table crammed with food, china and stemware glistening under the huge dining-room lamp as if seeing these things for the first time, or as if he had lost his appetite. Through the open window he watched nightfall creep onto the patio, darkening the trees and lawn.

"You haven't suffered enough," Gloria said.

"But I'm afraid to suffer," Natán answered, realizing he sounded like a child.

"It's not a matter of being afraid or unafraid," Antonio said. "Suffering happens, or it doesn't happen. You don't have to look for it; but when it comes, you can't get away from it."

"What I admire is that the two of you have suffered greatly, and even so, you haven't grown embittered. Quite the opposite, I can see a certain peacefulness. In looking at you I don't even see something I've seen in other faces; and recently I've started observing the features of ..."

"Whose features?" Gloria asked.

"No one in particular—people you don't go out of your way to meet—but certain faces leave a mark on you, and they're everywhere, especially in places ... It's a long story, and I'd just as soon skip the details. The important thing is that you've learned how to give up."

On the darkened patio, crickets had started chirping. It was a simple language, an alphabet with just a few sounds.

"You mean, give up our son?" Antonio said. "To the contrary; our son is always with us."

"How?" Natán said, quite startled. "How is he with you?" Seeing the pained surprise in both of them, he hurried to add: "Of course, in your memory, I understand.... In your memory, right?"

"How else would it be, Natán?" Antonio said drily. Natán flushed. The glass of wine in his hand was shaking.

"Please excuse me, I don't know what I'm saying. These days I've been thinking brainless thoughts, almost as if I've been regressing to certain ideas we haven't considered for many years: questions of immortality, the deceptive impressions we get from our finite senses, Plato's cavern—remember, Antonio? That was one of your favorite subjects. I remember you reading *The Republic* in that cheap edition, with pages that kept falling out. I think the title page was blue...."

"I don't follow you, Natán."

"Of course you don't. I'm really an idiot these days—and in this condition of mine, I really shouldn't have come." Starting to get to his feet, he tipped his glass over; the wine ran like blood across the tablecloth. "Damn it! Now I've done everything!"

"It doesn't matter, don't worry about it," Gloria said, soaking up the wine with paper towels.

"Thank you—thank you for the meal," Natán said. He got up slowly, shaking. "Everything was delicious. Please excuse me. I have to leave now."

"Are you crazy?" Antonio said. "How can you go so soon? Anyway, you're coming to the lecture with us."

"Natán, please, take your seat. I'm just bringing the dessert. It's *coco rallado*. I made it myself. Now, please sit down."

"I got the impression I offended you."

"What the hell did you say that could offend us?" Antonio said with an asthmatic breath. "Have you totally lost it? You'll offend us if you leave."

Natán lowered his head and sat back down. He drank the remnant of wine in his glass, then pulled the wrinkled piece of paper out of his wallet and handed it to Antonio.

"It's a poem I found. Tell me what you think."

Antonio adjusted his eyeglasses and read it carefully. For a few minutes, only the noise of crickets in their hiding places dared disturb the solemn silence. Gloria had placed her hands on the table like someone expecting a guilty verdict.

"I like it," Antonio said, exhaling a sigh of relief. "So you've turned out a poet after all. I was always sure you would wind up writing verse. Your trying to become a sociologist was nonsense; you were always too much the idealist. I always said it, always. Go ahead and read it, Gloria."

"I didn't write that, I swear I didn't. I don't know who did. I found it on the floor of a sentry's cabin. It spoke to me, so I kept it."

"Always the modest one. I already told you I liked it. So when did you start writing?"

"I swear it's not mine! I found it by chance. It impressed me, maybe because in that particular spot I would never have expected to find a poem."

"It's also clear you've fallen in love," Antonio said. "Congratulations. I only hope you haven't chosen poorly, after waiting this long. It must have been a real thunderclap if it got you to write this poem."

"Actually he didn't write it," Gloria said. "It's by the English poet Keats. People think he wrote that one just before he died."

"How about that!" Antonio said, kissing his wife on the cheek. "I always thought I couldn't do better than to marry a literature teacher. Of course I know Keats, but I would never have guessed that that was his."

"Keats was a marvelous poet," Gloria said. "He was also a fine human being. He loved his brothers and took care of them like a father."

"So he loved his brothers," Natán said, his eyes dwelling on the big red spot.

"I have an anthology of his poems in English, quite complete," Gloria said. "I can lend it to you."

After dessert and coffee, whose delicious flavors did not quite erase the awkward scene from dinner, and while Gloria and Antonio were changing clothes, Natán sat on the porch with the book. The crickets' noisy concert had passed away; notes of a distant melody came across the silent yard. Lights from the nearest houses, yet rather dim, led Natán to think about the lonely intimacy of people like his friends who might have suffered the loss of dear ones and must nevertheless force themselves to eat, make jokes and even be kind to guests who behave as thoughtlessly as he had. He flipped through the book but couldn't concentrate on it. A cat at the edge of the porch had fixed him with shining eyes, as if trying to place him. Natán got up and went over to stroke the animal, which fled into the darkened, strongly aromatic plants of the garden.

The lecture on Teilhard took place in a hotel meeting room. The lecturer, a Cuban lady in her fifties, wore a black dress and also a face that showed her to be in mourning. "She has one of *those* faces," Natán thought on seeing her. She explained various theories of evolution in a quivering voice; illustrating them with slides that seemed to have come from a kindergarten course. From a nearby bar came the discordant harmonies of a mediocre jazz band. An old man in the audience interrupted the speaker to ask a question about extraterrestrials.

"I'm sorry, sir, we're talking about something entirely different," the lady said with kindness. "Master Teilhard neither upheld nor opposed the idea of other-worldly beings; he was simply not interested in the matter. His purpose was to show that humans, after a long process of perfecting themselves, integrating their cultures and focusing their collective consciousness, could reach a supreme state where they effortlessly perceive the principle of universal love, a state he called *the omega point:* from diversity, they find unity. I will get to that shortly. Now, will you please take your seat."

With an alarm clock's precision, the man interrupted her every five minutes. At one moment he left aside his measured tone and said:

"A mystic and a scientist would not ignore the lives of other planets—lives that are directly linked with ours. Listen to me carefully, madam, and let everyone mark my words. Beware of fallacies. And I will not let myself be brushed off."

"We are talking about something entirely different here," the lady said again, with an increasing tremor in her voice as she addressed the old man. "I ask that you be so kind as to take your seat."

"I'm not sitting down, I'm going," he said, and muttering under his breath he quit the premises.

As the woman explained the omega point and showed the corresponding slide, a child's drawing that vaguely resembled a sunset, a trumpet in the bar hit an ugly high note; and Natán, sitting with his friends in the last row—they had gotten there late, and the room was inexplicably full—could scarcely make out the ramblings of that voice, in which he could hear a suppressed weeping. When she spoke the final words, a statement about harmony and divinity, and the public gave a gracious applause, the woman's eyes filled with tears. Someone in the crowd supplied a handkerchief. A young man next to Natán took a small flask out of his pocket and drank discreetly, but with gusto; obviously alcohol. Natán quickly said goodnight to Antonio and Gloria, excusing himself for an appointment. He wouldn't have been able to shake the hand of that lecturer or gaze into that familiar face.

Back home, he found Teresa's voice on his answering machine.

"I would have enjoyed seeing you. I'm taking the girls to my mom's house for the weekend. I had a huge argument with Felipe."

Was it love he felt for the woman? he asked himself as he listened to the message. He had largely forgotten what the word meant—the feelings it produced, the symmetries it contained. Was it dependency, need, possession, or just a phase that came and went without leaving a trace?

His father, or so he had gathered from relatives and friends in Cuba, had been a man forever in love; and his ties to Cuba's socialist regime were apparently marked by the same emotional traits. Perhaps, Natán thought, the ability to give oneself, to a woman, faith or ideal, was an inborn gift, a thing one couldn't learn; and a thing he had failed to inherit. On his desk he ran across the letter he had begun several times and never finished, with its twisted lines and telling spots of ink. The distance between himself and his father—a distance that started as soon as he could use his faculty for reason—had grown far too wide with the passage of years for any letter to bridge. He also knew that in any letter he wrote to his father, he should make at least a brief mention of José's existence; and who knew whether José existed?

For now the lake and forest had gone back to their habitually lonely state, as he saw by drawing the curtain one more time, an act that in recent days had given him a sinking feeling. He placed the photo on the desk and inspected it under a lamp. The slender piece of cardboard was ablaze with life. If José bore such a striking resemblance to their father, then he probably had, or had had, the old man's capacity for feeling. Gabriel Perdomo had said that José used to lash himself, "but not with a conventional whip." Natán well recalled that striking phrase. Of course poor Gabriel was crazy. Alicia, for her part, had said her nephew was "love through and through." His ex-lovers gave contradicting images of him. In all these differing impressions, the single point of agreement about this evasive man, who did not stop looking into the camera's lens with indifference, or perhaps with melancholy, was his intensity.

Natán took up the book of Keats and paused to reflect on some odes. He especially liked the first line of a sonnet: "Bright star, would I were stedfast as thou art—." He read the whole poem out loud. He'd forgotten the sense of calm that always came to him from reciting. Out of doors, in the distance, he heard laughing. It might be a nocturnal bird. He sat down on the balcony floor, inhaling the humid breezes that ran through the close-knit branches. No, he wouldn't write to his father. Why try to "tie up loose ends," to stanch old wounds, ask or grant forgiveness, feign an appearance of harmony, when the matter was cut-and-dried? The son had never loved his father, and the father had never loved his son. The day Natán left Cuba, the two had shaken hands without looking in each other's eyes, their fingers and hands cold with sweat—a pair of nervous men, full of shame at what brought them together and what was driving them far apart. The best they could have between them was common courtesy: borrowing money or returning it, making a present of a watch or a shirt, grabbing lunch or a glass of wine.

Natán had harbored the hope that his half-brother might be the missing link between them. Indeed, that seemed to be the old man's idea in asking him to take up the search; but the train of mysteries kept father out of the picture, exiled in a remote darkness, impossible to grasp or know, like the distant laugh of a man or a bird sounding through the pines.

He opened up the folding chair and fell backward onto it, face to those very stars that supposedly ordained the facts and mishaps of his life. This evening, Natán could not imagine how they might have any relation to his past, present or future. Maybe they were symbols of a desire beyond his reach, "if I were stedfast as thou art"—or maybe they were simply luminous objects, far from the pettiness, disappointment or pleasure that made up his daily comings and goings—*his*, Natán's; and, bathed in the refreshing silence of outdoors, he just fell asleep.

SEVEN

David, ciego y vidente. Con los ojos del alma verá dentro de tí.
David, blind psychic. The spirit's eye sees deeper.

The placard in two languages, dully colored letters on a whitish background, stuck out from the overgrown lawn of a rundown house in an alleyway of Liberty City, an impoverished black neighborhood in the very heart of Miami.

Natán, who had vowed not to waste another penny on these sessions, was arrested by the sign and stopped his car next to a cracked sidewalk, not far from a store where a group of black people, wearing unfriendly expressions, drank beer and played cards under an awning. Through this quiet scene ran a palpable tension, underlined by the heat of a cloudy afternoon. In several tenements, charred ruins showed the aftermath of a huge fire. The earth, severely burnt, had not recovered from the all-devouring flames; a few meandering blades of grass had fought to grow among the darkened, ruined bricks. Only the plants around the placard seemed to be thriving; shrubs and weeds were almost hiding the house.

In his novel attitude of giving in to destiny, a posture not quite free from defiance, Natán had been strolling around Miami's shantytown districts with the idea of exploring unknown places, and ignoring the danger of being assaulted. He got out, locked his car, gave a friendly greeting to the bystanders, who returned grimaces, then he crossed the overgrown garden and knocked loudly at the faded door.

"Come in, come in, the door is open," a woman's voice, obviously Hispanic, answered in English.

"Is David there?" Natán asked in Spanish.

"*Pase, pase.*" Now in Spanish, the lady kept inviting him to enter.

The door opened and he saw a strapping black man, age hard to tell, with sunglasses and reddish hair, dressed in a blue kimono. His smiling face had the blind person's indefinite expression.

"Are you David?"

"I am David, David," the man said, his falsetto voice bearing no relationship to his powerful body, sounding more like a ventriloquist's. "What is your name?"

"Natán. I don't know if you're still working, it's after five. How much do you charge?"

"Come in, Natán, come in. I don't work, I have no hours, I don't charge. I help those in need, it's not a job and I do it at any hour. If you are in need, and I think you are, then I'm here to help you, no strings attached. If you want to make a contribution afterward, I leave it to your conscience, only to your conscience. Please come in and sit down."

They were in the midst of a gigantic room, poorly lit by a ceiling lamp that was missing nearly all its bulbs. Thick curtains covered the windows, blocking the daylight. The furnishings were a chair in front of a huge, filmy mirror, an armchair set up on a kind of dais—a second-hand throne, Natán thought—and a large table with flowers, herbs, statuettes, platters of fruit and glasses of water. The house's interior walls had been knocked down to enlarge the room, which was permeated by an intense odor of basil.

"Please, have a seat in the chair," David said. "Make yourself comfortable."

"This is a temple, isn't it?" Natán asked.

With some difficulty, the man got up on the stand, then sprawled on the armchair and answered with his unwavering smile:

"The spirit likes a sense of space, of space; and so do I. Please excuse me if I put myself in this spot, a little higher than you. From here I'm better able to read your aura."

"I hope it's not so strong that it knocks you over," Natán joked; for, despite feeling cowed by the gloominess of the place and the man's wild aspect, he had begun to look on all of this as comical.

"Obviously you're Cuban," the man said with a laugh. "Your accent and your sense of humor are quite unmistakable."

"Yes, I'm Cuban. Aren't you, too?"

"I was born in the Dominican Republic but I lived in Cuba for a long time, during the fifties. I've also lived in Puerto Rico and Venezuela. I'm a citizen of the Caribbean, which is one big nation. How lovely the Caribbeans are! But more than that I hold myself a citizen of the world; this world and the other, you see? The other world, the world that has no governments, no conflicts, no poverty."

Muffled cries, like animal moans, came from behind a folding screen at the other end of the room.

"What's going on?"

David leaned forward and whispered like an accomplice:

"Those, my son, those are the sounds of love. I hope they don't disturb you." He paused and resumed in a rather stilted tone:

"I can speak familiarly with you, can't I? From your voice I take you for a thirty- or forty-year-old, and I'm seventy, although people tell me I don't look it. What I mean is, we're two adults and we can speak like adults. My sister's granddaughter is in my bed with her fiancé, her boyfriend, her husband—her man. She comes to see me every day, she helps me with chores, takes care of me. She has the right to pleasures that I, because of my age and calling, don't enjoy. From the moment you knocked at the door, I knew you weren't going to take offense; and I didn't want to interrupt them, I told them to carry on, since you would understand. That's what I told them: 'If he's coming to see me, he'll understand.' And now I can see you have the aura of a generous person, most generous, though also tormented, extremely tormented. They don't bother you, do they? Listen to how they give themselves to each other, they don't care about anything else. That's love—youth—life. Hearing them gives pleasure to me, and also to the spirits who are with me, to the spirits too. We take pleasure in others' pleasure, just as we are saddened by others' sadness. And you, despite your sense of humor, are a very sad man. Do you see yourself in that mirror?"

Natán looked at the reflecting glass beside the rostrum, and it showed not just him but the entire room; even the shadowy region at the far side, and the folding screen behind which the two youngsters were having a fine time.

"Do you see yourself? Then have a good look, straight on, without flinching. People need to look at themselves every now and then. I have my face etched in my mind; and I've never seen myself, because I've been blind since birth, but my inner mirror is always close at hand. Without that, I wouldn't be who I am. Have a good look, Natán. What do you see?"

Natán looked at himself with scorn.

"Obviously I'm not happy. No happy person would come to see a fortune-teller."

David laughed rather faintly.

"Fortune-teller I am not! Fortune-teller I am not! A clairvoyant is what I am, Natán. God takes away from you and gives you something else. It's the law, the law of mercy. No one understands it, nor do I. I can't see you with my eyes, but for that very reason I see you more clearly. The physical realm has no importance. Even so, I'm sad that at your age you've already had your hair go white."

An electric shock went through Natán's body.

"Why do you say white hair? What else do you see? I don't have white hair—not a single strand. Why do you say I have white hair?"

"That's the message I received. Ideas or messages come to me. In physical things I sometimes make mistakes, I often make mistakes."

"Where did you get that message? Try to tell me. Don't worry about whether you were mistaken. Try to tell me. It's very important."

The man took off his glasses. His errant, misshapen eyes, covered with scars, lent a ferocious aspect to that calm and cheerful face. Natán wanted to turn away, but something irresistible in the gaze that wasn't a gaze kept him looking.

"What are you seeking, my son? What torments you so? You can trust in me, open your heart to me. What is your torment?"

"You are the one who should be telling me," Natán said like a willful youngster without moving his eyes from the man's face, unlike any he'd seen.

David put on his glasses once more. The moans of the couple had intensified, they were now almost screams, and rather than pleasure they sounded like torture. In the mirror Natán could see the screen give a jolt, while the bed springs quivered like a death rattle.

"They enjoy themselves, and you suffer," David said softly. "That's what you're thinking. Isn't it what you're thinking?"

"No. I'm thinking about why you said I had white hair. If you really do see into the occult, you should be able to tell me about those messages of yours."

The man kept silent. Behind the screen, too, an apparent calm had settled, broken only by light clicking sounds that were probably kisses. David's lips were moving ever so slightly, as if he were praying to himself. At last he said:

"Signals come to me. You have a wall around you that doesn't let me see you clearly, it doesn't let me see you; but I feel the spirits around me are uneasy, they're pacing back and forth, they're acting wounded, and one of them wants to cry. Woman of darkness, go in peace! Go down, with your wounds, to the bottom of the well! Go, noble virgin, go and don't return! And you, sweet boy, peace be with you! Suckle gently at the breast of your holy mother, who is our protector! Do you believe in vampires, Natán?"

"I don't know."

"The day is full of celestial beings, but the night is full of demons. Day and night are the same to me, so I can feel them at the same time, the same time. Someone wants to drink your blood. He's hovering over you. You have to show him you feel no fear, no fear. Bad spirits are like dogs, they leave you alone if they find you at peace, but if they see you in fear they tear you to pieces. Have some fruit—there, on the table. Have a piece of fruit."

"Which one?"

"Any one you want, any one you want."

It struck him as ludicrous, but Natán was too frightened not to obey, so he took a pear.

"Do you have somewhere I can wash this?" he asked timidly, holding the fruit as if it were a stick of dynamite.

"Which one did you take?"

"A pear."

"Bad choice; but it's too late, you can't change it. The pear is a weak fruit, insignificant. Don't worry, it's better than nothing. Eat it with faith in your heart. Faith is everything."

"Which one should I have chosen?"

"It doesn't matter. If you want to wash it, since I see you're fastidious, and that's a part of your problem, a big part of your problem, the bathroom is in the back, near the bed."

Natán hesitated.

"But then I will have to go close to them."

"So what? It doesn't matter to them at all, not at all. Love is that way, it's higher than anyone or anything. And now they love each other. They're really in love."

Their panting, which had once more found its frenetic rhythm, seemed to say so.

"No, no, I can't. It embarrasses me."

"Then go to the patio. You've got a spigot on the wall, near the door. It's here, in back of me."

Outdoors, clouds obscured the last minutes of daylight. A light rain cascaded over the shrubs, over cages with hens and rabbits, discarded scraps of metal, broken furniture now covered in moss, and a small, ruined boat next to which three goats were sleeping. While Natán tried opening the spigot, he thought these animals might be for sacrificing; their innocent blood might be spilt to appease the whims or fury of heartless beings; and the fruit he was about to eat, as harmless as it might seem, could have been injected with venom. The blind David, besides being a clairvoyant, might also be a madman or a procurer. Perhaps that relative and her lover, groaning behind a screen, were just a prostitute and customer, united in a commercial exchange under the auspices of the blind man. The pear might be drugged.

A shadow passed quietly across the back of the patio: a man in a hat and raincoat walked alongside a fence and paused under a luxuriant tree that the gathering darkness had made even grander. Natán dropped the pear, hurried around the house, whose windows were blockaded by the heavy curtains, and went out to the street under a drizzle that quickly became a downpour.

Before starting the car, Natán threw a glance at the photo. The man who looked like his father had grown opaque, a portrait decayed by time, in sharp contrast to the image of the old lady, who remained as vivid as before. A black youngster knocked at the car window and gestured wildly; he wanted to sell or get something. Natán shook his head and drove away at full speed, turning into streets full of puddles, dodging potholes, rounding deserted corners, shooting past nearly invisible houses, hardly able to read the numbers of avenues, finding his way by the silhouettes of skyscrapers.

By the time the storm had abated, he had already crossed the railway line that divided northwest Miami from the industrial zone of Hialeah. At moments he thought he heard a voice clearly pronouncing his name: "Natán!" It was neither a shout nor a whisper, not an urgent call or a greeting, but more like a command, spoken with an emphasis that seemed to say, "Come!" or "Turn around!" or "Stop!"

The first time he heard it, he was waiting at a traffic light; and it was so clear that he almost asked, "What?" The voice was coming from the air, from the rain, from the incipient night; it sounded quite close by, abrupt and peremptory. "Natán!"

"Nobody is calling me," he reassured himself. "No one can be calling me."

A pair of prostitutes, who had taken shelter in a doorway with a razed roof, crossed in front of his car with a big fuss, moving like dancers. One cried out: "Yourself!"

Natán stepped on it. The voice rose up from behind his head, as if a passenger in the rear had leaned forward and said to him: "Natán! Natán!"

"Leave me alone!" Natán said, hitting the seat with his fist.

Then he heard it from a distance, as from someone in a hurry to catch up with him. He told himself to ignore it.

The fourth time, however, as he crossed the desolate neighborhood of factories and warehouses with their empty parking lots and sturdy fences behind which dogs were barking incessantly, Natán decided to get out of the car and call Teresa from a public phone. It was full night, and the downpour had put a biting humidity into the nocturnal breeze. With awkward, obstinate movements, through a flood of water on the roadway, a bum was pulling a metal cart from one sidewalk to another. Boxes and tree branches were floating pell-mell in the darkened stream.

"Is your husband there?" Natán asked when Teresa answered with sleep in her voice.

"It's you!" Her voice perked up. "I almost never hear you on the phone, but you sound the same. No, Felipe just went out with some of his buddies and he'll come home drunk. Is something going on?"

"I need to see you. I'm on the road. I'll be home in fifteen minutes."

Teresa paused. "I'll call my mom to see if I can leave the girls with her. I'll tell her I have a headache and I need to rest."

"I'll be waiting for you."

"What's going on with you?"

"With me? Nothing. I'll be waiting."

He was about to hang up when, coming from the handset, he heard that same robust and masculine voice.

"Close to you, Natán, close to you."

"Teresa? Teresa?" Natán, looking all round, put the phone to his face like someone pressing a revolver there. "Is it you, Teresa?"

The connection broke up and the drone of an empty phone line buzzed in his ear.

At home, when he switched on the lights, Natán suddenly feared that he must have opened the wrong door. In the stillness of his rooms, the furniture, books and clothing all seemed to be alive with a mysterious resonance, like signals guiding a stranger who looks for something or someplace he's never seen. A few minutes elapsed before he could see that this really was where he had lived for more than a year, and that these things around him were the same ones he'd bought over time: the dark green sofa, the bookshelf, lamps, paintings, dining table with its glossy varnish, the unmade bed.

And then he realized he was the one who had changed; and he might never again experience the relief he had always felt when he crossed his threshold on returning from work or shopping or visiting or strolling: the well-being of a man who, with some effort, has found a congenial place to hang his hat. Could it be he had never actually felt that sense of ease? He didn't remember. He couldn't imagine how his life had been only three months earlier. He had lost something, perhaps something irreplaceable; but what?

The rain got worse again, making a thick curtain across the landscape on the other side of his glass door, leaving one to imagine the uproar that the storm had to be raising on the surface of the lake. He could make out the boats pitching violently against the dock, as if shaken by angry arms.

Natán went into the shower, hoping to wash away the gloominess that had descended on him—the fear that had been dogging him since his visit to the clairvoyant, whom he blamed for his state of mind, especially for the voice that kept calling his name and saying: *Close to you.*

"A warm bath will get rid of all this," he told himself out loud. "Mama always relied on a warm bath."

He surprised himself. "Mama" was a word he'd used as an infant. Later on, in a show of independence, he had addressed his mother by her given name, Esther; and so he had called her until the day she died. His mother, it seemed, had accepted that her son was hard, indifferent—someone for whom affection and mercy did not exist. Lucky for her, God was there to make up for all the failings of this world. And Natán resented that, too.

Whatever advice his mother gave he held in contempt, deriding it as uneducated drivel, rooted in folk wisdom, shot through with superstition; but as he felt the warm water stream over his body and vapor get into his pores, he granted that on this one subject his mother was quite right.

Teresa came in at ten, soaked from head to foot, shy and smiling, with an ungainly hairstyle that the water had completely undone.

"You scared me. Every time you call it's because you're sick. Do you feel ill?"

Natán lowered his head in shame, but then, when he looked into those innocent eyes that would never see him fully, he said with heart:

"If I felt ill, now I feel better for seeing you"—and, taking up her delicate arm: "You're dripping. Let me dry you off."

"The bathroom is what I need. I'll just take a shower."

"Good idea. Nothing is better than a shower."

Natán sat down on the edge of the bed while Teresa, under the stream of water, crooned something in English he'd never heard. He turned off the lamp on the night table and leaned his head against the pillow, trying to make out the words of the song. His eyes were closing when a noise brought him up. In the back of his closet, something had moved. Not something, someone; it was a man. He had camouflaged himself behind the racks of clothing, taken shelter in the dark. Natán could feel the man's gaze from behind the open door of the narrow closet, which was as deep as a room. He couldn't make out the intruder's profile from among the darkened shapes of his own dress suits, shirts, shoes and other items. That hat sticking out of a corner—was it the one he had bought on a whim during a recent visit to New York, or was it the one he had just seen on the blind man's patio, covering a stranger's head? He got to his feet. He must see if his mind was playing tricks on him. He moved a few feet and stopped. No, better to stay where he was—but why? He should go in, have a good look, face it.

Teresa came out of the bathroom half-dressed, scrubbing her hair. Natán hugged her, without taking his eye from the unmoving line of clothes. "I can turn on the light and expose you," Natán silently told the trapped shadow that still seemed to be watching him.

"Hey, let me be," Teresa said softly. "Come on, let me loose. Is this what you called me for?"

"No, for something else," Natán said, kissing her. "But I forgot what it was."

"Let me dry myself," Teresa said, smiling and answering his kisses. "Go ahead and turn on the light."

"Better with the light off," he said, quite roused by her damp flesh and the fragrance of her wetted hair, as by the new experience of doing it in front of an onlooker. "Let's get on the bed."

"I'm going to get your sheets wet!" she protested.

"Doesn't matter."

Natán usually approached sex with an extended roundabout of

kisses and caresses, especially with a woman for whom he felt a soft spot; but now he was driven to take her at once, to seize hold of that body which always gave itself with gentleness, and his violent entry provoked a cry of pain and surprise from Teresa, who tried to protect herself by pushing him away, even by scratching his arms. At last, convulsed with sobs, she admitted him with quick, short movements to blunt the force of penetration.

Submerged in moisture, his hands going everywhere, engrossed in touching and rubbing, aroused by the pain he inflicted, as well as by the pleasure of parading his manliness before the visitor, Natán was so caught up in his frenzy that he didn't feel the usual impulse to finish, and he saw he could stay hard for a good long time inside this woman who clearly did not enjoy his embrace. Lashes of rain and the din of thunder went with her muffled groans. "Look at me," Natán thought as he twisted and turned without letup, charging with brutal movements that made Teresa cry out again and again. "Mark me well. I can do what you can't."

At last Natán felt his inner strength focus, with lively intensity, on the liquid that spilled out with a liberating energy; but on leaving Teresa's body, sweating and exhausted, he was again overcome with fear.

In the darkness of the room, he could feel the approach of the mysterious person who, it seemed, had just decided to leave his hiding place. He thought he could hear someone's halting breath, but after a few minutes he realized it was his own. He stayed perfectly still, keeping himself in check, nervously watching every corner of the room.

"All you're doing is using me," he heard Teresa say. "It's not what I'm made for. That's not me. It isn't."

Natán enfolded his lover's shoulders in his arms, also seeking protection.

"Don't say that."

"Maybe I shouldn't care. In a way, I use you too; but it's different, because I love you."

"Teresa, we love each other."

"It frightens me."

"What do you know about fear?"

"I know more than you do."

"How do you mean?"

"I have two daughters and a husband. I'm frightened of myself, of what I do. I don't want to lose my daughters. They're my life. And maybe, after all, I don't want to lose my husband. No matter our troubles, we have many years together, he's a good man; he's just a bit of a brute, and he drinks a little more than he should."

"Don't worry, you won't lose anybody. And you won't lose me, either. What else frightens you?"

"Oh, lots of things."

"Like what?"

"I don't know—lots of things. Why do you want to hear them?"

"It's important. Let's make a deal. For every one of your fears that you tell me, I'll tell you one of mine."

"My fears keep changing. When I was a girl I was afraid of a neighbor, a lady whose house was falling down. Her sons and husband had died in a train wreck. She lived all alone, completely alone. She didn't want to see anybody. She had a cousin, a girl who brought her food on the weekends, and that was her only visitor. At night she went out on her patio with a candle, she walked in circles and spoke to herself or prayed, and at times she hit her fist into a tree; I remember the tree, it was a *flamboyán*. One time she went out naked. Her hair was down to her knees. I watched her from behind the kitchen door of our house, and I was scared to death. On a morning some years afterward, they found her hanging dead from the *flamboyán*. She was thin, so thin, wasted away. Poor woman! I was so frightened of her, and now I know she was just a poor, harmless woman who should have aroused my pity, and not my fear! But fears are like that, they're beyond explanation. I was just a girl, I didn't understand."

"And you never saw her again?"

"What?"

"That woman—you never saw her again?"

"How would I have seen her? She was dead."

"So you don't believe that dead people reappear? You've never experienced the supernatural?"

Natán had closed his eyes in order not to look at the shadow that seemed to be gliding along the wall.

Teresa answered in a faint voice. "I don't know whether they reappear or not. I believe they do. When I was fourteen, I was sure I had seen my grandmother in the doorway of our house—my father's mother, who had died shortly before. It could have been a dream, because I was thinking about her a great deal. Anyway, I wasn't scared. I saw her as something natural rather than supernatural—do you understand? How strange, I thought, my grandmother is here, but she's dead. It's definitely my sweet grandmother. I didn't ask why. She must have surprised me, but she certainly didn't frighten me. What about you? What are you scared of?"

Without opening his eyes, Natán said: "I was always afraid of places I didn't know. When I was a boy we moved often, my father was always going here and there, changing houses, changing towns—he couldn't be happy in one place. Every new house was frightening to me. I was scared to think of what must have gone on there before we arrived; I kept imagining the horrible things that must have happened in my own room. The walls and ceilings frightened me. Almost as soon as I could feel at home, Father told us we were moving again. Mother and I had to follow him like lambs to the slaughter—and in the new place, my fear started up again. That's how it was."

"If you'd had a brother, you might not have been frightened. Your brother would have kept you company."

"Well, yes, you're right; with a brother I wouldn't have felt fear. How ironic!"

"I don't get the irony."

"You can't. It's really complicated. I always wanted a brother."

"You haven't been able to find him, have you?"

"Who?"

"The one you've been trying to find, your half-brother. José, isn't it?"

"José. I didn't find him. I stopped trying. It doesn't interest me. I forgot all about it. A ridiculous story—I'm sure he doesn't live in Miami. His aunt told me he traveled a lot. Once he sent her a postcard from Argentina. When you get out of Cuba you see the world is huge, and you can go anywhere. What else frightens you?"

"Spiders and scorpions."

"For me it's serpents, snakes, or whatever crawls"—and with that, Natán opened his eyes. He couldn't make out the shadow anywhere in the room. He sat up and threw a glance into the closet. When he saw it was perfectly still, he put his head back on the pillow next to Teresa's.

"I'm afraid of the sea at night," she said.

"For me it's quite the opposite. I love to swim in the nighttime sea. Once my dad rented a house next to a pier in Santa Cruz del Sur. We lived there for two months. He and I went to swim before dawn, and we weren't afraid of sharks or anything else. My father was a great swimmer in those days—probably still is—well, he's old and sick. Maybe he can't swim as before."

"I'm afraid of illnesses," Teresa said. "I mean, of a serious illness that would leave me infirm. And I'm afraid of old age. It's a terrible thing, old age."

"The worst thing is to be young and one day wake up old," Natán said. "But getting old is a gradual process, you get accustomed to it. I can feel myself getting old, but it doesn't worry me. What I do fear is being old *and* lonely. My mother was a lonely old woman. My father is a lonely old man. My mother was afraid, and so is my father, even if he doesn't say so. In his last letter, fear was easy to read between the lines."

They kept silence together for a short time. Natán imagined that the invisible presence had withdrawn, perhaps defeated by the current of feeling that ran between Teresa and himself. That idea swelled his head in a childish way; but it wasn't mere boasting, or so he told himself, it was an instinct of self-affirmation: an affirmation of life. The act of talking about fear with the woman lying at his side had made his own fear go away—or had made it less intense.

"What about death?" she asked. "Aren't you afraid to die?"

"I don't understand death. I can't imagine it. And one is not afraid of things one can't imagine."

"I would say the opposite. You get frightened of those things you can't imagine."

Natán turned to inspect the profile of this woman whom he had, without a doubt, undervalued.

"You could be right, Teresa. It's fantastic, what you said about your grandma. How did you see that visit as natural? Didn't you get scared? Didn't you tell yourself this is a ghost, and ghosts can hurt you?"

"I don't remember exactly what I was thinking. It's been a long time. I must have felt it natural for her to be there because she loved me. Probably I supposed that even after she died she would want to stay close to her family, to people she had always loved. It must have seemed natural to me. A ghost, as we think of it, is something with no relation to living people; but this was my grandmother who had pampered me, given me beautiful gifts, hugged and kissed me so many times. And she seemed so real, in the same robe she used to wear after a bath. As I say, I don't really remember what I was thinking, but I remember the robe and yellow flowers—I think they were sunflowers. I think she also had on some perfume. Crazy, isn't it? My mother was terrified when I told her the story. She told me to forget it. She said she couldn't bear the idea that her daughter might be turning into a medium. They say people are born with that ability, but if they don't practice it they lose it. My mother hated spiritualism, because my grandmother—I mean my mother's mother, not the one I saw in the doorway—had been a famous spiritualist. They forced my mother to go to the séances. That grandmother died before I was born, but my aunts used to tell stories. For me spiritualism was no big deal, I never went to a session, I never gave a thought to it then or now. I've always preferred things you can touch. In this, I think I'm an average woman—in this and everything else. I've had some education, in Cuba I was a good student, then in Spain my aunt and uncle made me go for a higher degree, but I never graduated; I'm not a person of education and culture, as you are."

"You're not average, and I'm neither educated nor cultured. Anyway, what do those words mean? You're special; at least you are to me. It's true I've studied and read books, but in the end it doesn't mean much. Simplicity and sincerity count for a lot more. I'm afraid of lies. That's another of my fears: the lie. In Cuba for so many years I lived among people who lied. Lying was everywhere; from morning to night all you heard were lies, lies, lies."

Teresa got up from the bed and started to dress.

98

"I'm also afraid of lies," she said as she buttoned her blouse. "That's why I told you I'm afraid of myself. That's what I'm doing here: lying. I tell lies to my husband, my mom, my kids. I'm lying to the whole world. I'm a liar."

"That's different. You and I love each other. Love can make anything right. At times the truth can be hurtful, and it's better to keep silent."

"You don't need to defend me. At bottom you don't really value me because you know I lie."

"Please," Natán said, "let's not spoil this."

Teresa turned on the light, and at once the intimacy that lived between them had run out of the room—a room where ghosts could no longer strike fear, but where companionship and pleasure also had no place. The bed-sheets were spotted with sweat. In his closet, the clothes hung silent and useless.

"I'm off," she said.

"Don't go yet. Don't leave this way. It makes me sad. Just stay a minute more."

"I've got to go. I have to get the girls from my mom before Felipe comes back."

Natán put on his shoes while Teresa fixed her hair in the mirror. "Can I show you something?" he said. "It's a photo—a photo of Alicia, the aunt of my half-brother. Here."

Overcoming his impulse to check for the other figure, he handed it to her.

Teresa smiled.

"What a lovely old woman! She looks like my mother's cousin, a spinster who lives in Galicia. They say that as a youngster she was the prettiest girl in town. And who is this man?"

Natán swallowed. "The man? That's my half-brother. He looks just as my father did at that age."

99

"He also looks a bit like you." Teresa looked at Natán and then at the photo. "I can see a family resemblance."

"Do you?"

"Most certainly—eyes, nose, a bit of the face. He's very handsome. The white hair flatters him, gives him an interest. He's very natty."

"My father was also quite good-looking. I was the ugly duckling."

"Fine! That means no one else will look at you; besides me, I mean. When did she give you the photo?" Teresa said, handing it back.

"A few days ago." He glanced at the two images—well defined, spotlessly clear—and put the photo on his dresser.

Teresa made a sound between a breath and a cough. She took out her compact and lipstick and made herself up with rapid movements, looking into the small mirror with disapproval. *She's no beauty,* Natán thought, *but she's the one for me.*

"I'm going. Don't kiss me or anything like that."

From his bedroom window, he watched her walk away between cars that shone in the rain; a small, downcast woman, slightly hunched over by her burden of guilt. Her hair fell on her shoulders with a certain feeling of grief, moistened by the stubborn rain. Her hurried step looked like a fugitive's gait. Twice she glanced up but made no signal. Maybe she was looking at the overcast sky, or at the tops of the trees that surrounded his building.

Mechanically Natán cleaned the ashtrays, dusted the furniture, swept the floor, washed the dishes and scrubbed the bathroom tiles. He didn't want to keep still.

The voice has gone away, and him too.

He thought of turning on the TV to get the latest news from Iraq and Kuwait, where , according to the radio report he had heard that morning, allied forces were on the brink of victory; but then he realized he had no interest in the wars of this world, at least not tonight, when for the first time in a while he could feel an inner peace that had no relationship to the surface of things.

Nor did he want to pull back the curtain and look toward the lake; for he was certain that nobody would be wandering about on the other shore.

That night he slept with the photo of Alicia and José under his pillow, like someone clutching an amulet to chase away bad spirits or insomnia or sorrow; or to ward off, now and forever, the visits of unwelcome beings.

CHAPTER

EIGHT

Early the following week, Natán received two unexpected letters.
The first, postmarked in Naples, Florida, was from Gabriel
Perdomo.

Mr. Natán Velázquez
Miami (THE ACCURSED)

Aware of a calling that demands rejection of all fickleness
and vanity in this world, with its conventions whose only
aim is to obscure the real question, namely, the hatred humans practice—at times openly, giving rise to crime, wars,
theft, rape, betrayal, calumny, blackmail, fraud and all the
other vile stuff that fills and animates newspapers and radio
and TV, which are themselves governed by a deadly hatred of
their rivals (that is to say, themselves) and at times covertly,
as in the lures that politicians use to trap their victims, and
I mean politicians of every stripe—leftists, rightist, centrists,

democrats, dictators, even the new crowd of ecologists—
and the lures that priests, churchmen, prophets and spiritual counselors hold out under the guise of worshipping
what they wrongly call God, and on top of that the snares of
ordinary, average people with sophisms less offensive, though
no less fatal, about family ties, blood ties, intimate liaisons
or pure friendship—which is a myth, as if the fate of others
really mattered—all of it justified by duties of kinship, supposed congeniality, passing desire (as desire must be), poorly
named affinities or common interests that don't exist, when
in truth the only common interest or affinity is hatred, or in
most cases a twisted drive to possess, manipulate and enslave, upheld at times by pleasing and venerable maxims,
the most renowned of these being *Love thy neighbor as thy-
self,* which history attributes to Jesus, of whom one may
only say that if he actually lived he was a man like any other,
who founded a sect with himself in the center and followers
who loved him blindly, and such is, I repeat, the goal all
men greater or lesser are thrown to pursue—that people
blindly love them even if this adoration is a mask for hate—
and when I say men I naturally mean men and women, young
and old, all we may call sentient beings, assuming that animals do not form part of this hideous conglomerate of hatred, and again I repeat, *HATRED, ODIO,* in capital letters,
English and Spanish, the two languages I know, although I
suppose this must be true for every human language, I know
for example that the word in French is *haine* as one may
learn by consulting a dictionary but that is really beside the
point and anyway, in this place where they have confined me
with HATE we naturally do not have dictionaries, because
part of the plan is to change the meaning of each and every
word so that language, instead of being a means to commu-

nicate, becomes an instrument of deformation and there I should say they have gained an almost total triumph, but insofar as a single person in this world may yet refuse to speak in corrupted words then language itself will keep its value, and in vain will they build prisons with bars or fences or prisons disguised as rest homes, with beautiful gardens, like this one near Naples where they recently transferred me because my family, my accursed family, wants to imprison me in a golden cage where I eat with silverware, everything paid with money gained from enslaving others through decades of indignity, cheating and swindling and paying rotten salaries to people they see as inferior, despite their voicing— my relatives, *accursed ones*—lofty ideals of love and benevolence, and despite their giving with great gestures to charitable institutions in Cuba and the United States they were always the utmost exemplars of hypocrisy, kings and queens of farce, from my plantation-owning great-grandfather who was a whoremonger and died of syphilis despite going to church every Sunday with my poor great-grandmother—just another slave, from what I remember of her and from family stories, a slave even though endowed with fabulous wealth, so people never saw her abasement—then my grandfather inherited the fortune along with the degradation, the avarice that makes a shambles of everything, and he was like Midas, everything he touched turned to gold, then my father and uncles carried on the tradition as faithful heirs, of course they didn't plan on Fidel Castro and his socialism or communism which is another face of the same coin, all that wealth simply passed from the wealthy to Castro's people and after two or three successes applauded by the masses, above all by the malcontents and resentful ones who are primarily moved by envy and HATE—I say that after those acclaimed

successes like universal education and health care they then
imposed a police state, Jacobin terror, hypocrisy, denunciation, opportunism and blackmail took root as the new cur-
rency that conferred riches, or in other words money lost
value while hypocrisy, denunciation, servility, physical and
mental harassment gained in value, all this in hand with poverty spread by the state—I don't mean the reign of medioc-
rity because this has been in effect since the island was discovered—and my family fled to the United States not because they were better than the communists but because they
were suddenly faced with an enemy even mightier than they,
even more abject and twisted, and here, with money they
had stowed away, with various connections and the same
ability to cheat and enslave, and still keeping the Midas touch
that was part of their genetic makeup, through the passage
of years they raised an edifice of fame and vanity upheld by
banks—those gloomy deposits of blood, reaching to the
last drop of daily sacrifice—and of course by those ever-
present politicians whose smiles nonetheless do not allow
to show, in their glory, the sets of fangs that Dracula himself
would have envied, to such an extent that they now give
themselves the luxury of yanking me away from that hospital in Miami, where they locked me up to muzzle me, and
dragging me to this garden on a plain, watched over by blood-
thirsty police dressed up as doctors and nurses and even,
some of them, as administrators fit for a party in suits and
ties, except that this party is a cannibal's feast, but they are
not going to eat me. They will not taste my meat. They shall
not have my bones for making soup. No.

Aware, then, of my mission, which is to tell the truth and
only the truth, and to preach disinterest in a world where

everyone wants something from someone else, and where that something is predicated on the deepest HATE as well as on its siblings envy, ambition, the drive to possess and to enslave, and humanity's watchword, an ever-present and all-governing vanity—as I say, with a vivid awareness that my calling in this life is unrelated to the ridiculous ceremony of penning letters, I have chosen this recourse, which only serves to cheat and cajole and reproduce on paper the very drives I loathe, as a means to honor or perhaps gratify my deceased friend José Velázquez, who has come before me in my dreams and who with his customary tact, with shyness and above all with his wise faculty of detachment has refrained from asking anything of me—because José knew and still knows the emptiness of all things, unlike Solomon who dedicated proverbs and precepts to the young after he had spent a long life glutted on gold and lacked even the decency to set fire to his possessions or even to give them away, but was merely content to declaim *Vanity of vanities, All is vanity*—and perhaps, even as he sat writing those words, he had slaves working fans around him, perfumed women who waited to refresh him with lotions, and cooks, wretched, undervalued beings, toiling and sweating to concoct the delicacies that this great lord might fancy after his audacious dalliance with the written word, unlike José, who in his journey through this world took pains to be thoughtful and show respect, always from a distance, and not to offer advice or envelop with love, since love is only a stalking-horse for ill-natured passions that follow in its train, and who was the only person not to make fun of me but instead listened to me, paid heed to my judgments, understood and shared them, and on those few occasions when he spoke—since he liked listening above all, and I was grateful to him for that—it was merely to add an idea of his own that concurred with my thinking and, may I say in all humility, broadened and enriched it, to the point that enemies of the truth, people who uphold the reign of evil, unable to tolerate the existence of one who saw the light and supported someone with a mandate to denounce the humbug and iniquity that rule in this blood-soaked concentration camp by which I mean the whole world with no exceptions, not even lovely Switzerland, where victims feed on victims in an endless chain—I repeat, unable to regard with dispassion how the man who had been a scourge to them could count on a steadfast ally, they determined to do away with him by secret means that might have included the use of witchcraft, and it is not granted that I say anything more about it until the Day arrives. Now I've got to go for my meal.

Two hours later, I resume my statement whose only aim is to keep faith with the man I came to regard as my right hand, the deceased José Velázquez, and as I was saying before they summoned me to eat the swill they serve for food in this golden cage and force me to digest against my will, because even if I can be sure they would not think of poisoning me, for at bottom they are cowards, one never knows what they might do in a moment of despair, so for that reason I go very slowly and wait for ten or fifteen minutes after swallowing to see the reaction, as I know my stomach will tell me if poison is present, one must be *keen as a serpent and mild as a dove,* or so they say spoke the man called Jesus Christ, at times I recall his phrases and I say to myself *therein resides truth,* even if Christianity has provoked more evil than good, has divided families and nations and spilt more blood than any other faith, and aside from the bare numbers that one may consult in case of doubt and vindicate me from charges of blasphemy, in the Gospel one can read with perfect clarity, *Think not that I am come to send peace on earth, I came not to send peace but a sword,* and this according to his disciples is what the Master spoke, he himself stated this idea and one must commend his sincerity—that is, if he existed—and whoever might choose the serpent and the dove as examples to follow was truly correct, so with feigned indifference and innocence I very slowly eat the food that those *accursed ones* put on my plate every day, I eat slowly and wait a while and then I eat some more, this afternoon's menu was London broil, rice with almonds and carrots with a tart sauce, and I would have wanted to keep writing but they, the *accursed ones,* force me to eat and even watch to make sure I chew and swallow, as if I were a newborn, it's part of the abasement and insult but one day they will get their just desert, so I had to break off what I was saying about José, who appeared before me in a dream, not exactly as he was because in dreams the truth will show itself as from behind a curtain, but enough like him so I could have no doubts that this was he who had been my rock for many years, because even if we didn't see each other so often since he had to work, and besides he liked to travel here and there, perhaps as a way to flee from the vileness of humanity—which one can't escape, that much is clear—as I say, despite the distance and the months that went by without our meeting, I always knew I could count on him without conditions, and when in my dream I met that man who seemed to be walking along the bank of a river, I'm rather sure it wasn't the sea because I saw no shore but a rocky

ground that reached from a forest to the water, on seeing
him I knew it was José and I wanted to greet him, but as
happens in dreams I was motionless and without speech, he
turned quickly to me and said in a low voice *My poor brother*
and something else I don't remember, and I thought he was
calling me his brother because indeed that was how I had
come to see him, but then he said *My poor brother Natán*
and something else I can't recall, and when I woke up I
found the calling-card you had left when you visited me at
that jail in Miami *(the accursed)* and I realized José was talking about the hapless fellow who had come to ask me about
him, who told me he was his brother and was looking for
him, and of course on that occasion I didn't believe you
because people are cheats and they've fooled me many times
and I always like to verify things before I take them on their
face, but on hearing José say *My poor brother Natán* as he
walked near the water in that gloomy, tree-shaded spot I
knew you had not deceived me, although certainly you deceived me in other things because your face, if you excuse
me for saying so, is that of someone who has no worth and
therefore has to go through life telling lies, or to put it more
clearly you have a coward's face, I am able to read people's
eyes because aside from the fact that my calling, which is to
tell the truth, has obliged me to scrutinize and unmask everyone I encounter in my path, I possess the gift of pen-
etrating the most hidden regions of the soul and seeing the
garbage that's collected there, and in yours I must say I see
enough to stop up a well, and that may be why in my dream
I heard José exclaim *My poor brother* because he felt a great
sadness at the fact that you must go through life sunk in a
latrine with shit up to your collar, or probably he wanted in
some way to help you because José was a generous guy,

always thinking about others, he had nothing of his own, and whenever he had to help someone or give something away, no matter what, he did it without thinking, as if it were the most natural thing in the world—unlike my family, *the accursed ones,* who always did so with the idea of showing off or exercising power, and unlike the communists who parade their good works and love of justice even as they drink the people's blood and leave them as dry as bones in a desert—no, José was not like that, he gave of himself with complete disinterest and he forgot about the favors he did, indeed he exemplified the phrase they say Jesus spoke, *But when thou doest alms, let not thy right hand know what thy left hand doeth,* of course José didn't do it out of Christian doctrine but because he had a compassionate nature, and also, as I had taught him, he was deeply detached, because detachment alone is pure, and this I tell you, I Gabriel Perdomo, speaking on my own authority, José's ladies and girlfriends reproached him for being a spendthrift because he threw away his money at games of chance like dog-races or horse-races or cards or cock-fights but he didn't do it out of weakness or vice, he did it because giving in to games of chance is a way of expressing indifference, and I know that whatever he won he shared without further ado, those same women who demeaned him and made his life miserable were the first to gain whenever he had a lucky streak, José was free of egotism and for that very reason he felt like a rich man and he felt sorry for people like my family, *the accursed ones,* who are slaves to greed, always driven to get more, and the more they get the more they want, which is the hell of this earth, and it may be for this reason too that in my dream I heard him telling me *My poor brother,* because no one knows better than he that you are also a victim of voracity, and when you came to me at that jail in Miami *the accursed* I saw in you, apart from that profound cowardice I mentioned, a monstrous egotism that pulls you in like a chain, and this is something even more vile than the curse that Keats, one of José's favorite poets, described in his verse *Endymion* when he spoke of *a forlorn wretch, Doom'd with enfeebled carcase to outstretch His loathed existence through ten centuries, And then to die alone,* because José loved poetry but not the pettiness of present-day poets who go scouring the language for trivial effects, with their verses where one looks for meaning or sensibility and only finds word-games—José loved the poetry of bygone epochs that showed the grandeur and horror of this curious reptile we call the human being, and he read aloud to me from not only Keats but Quevedo, Novalis, Calderón of course and Shakespeare, not omitting Poe and Baudelaire, although at last I prevailed on him to forget about literature because long and short, no matter how fine it may be, one only sees in it the drunken pursuit of power by egomaniacal spirits who try to dominate people by means of rhymes and other verbal tricks that work like barbiturates, without giving pause to think that in the end there is no salvation, no salvation, *no salvation,* not in verses or novels or speeches or sermons or letters, much less in the repellent propaganda of capitalists or less of communists, for whom it seems the bell has already tolled, or still less in the sweetest pronouncements of so-called centrists or moderates, because they all aim for the submission of our free will through doctrines of property and superficial freedom— that's capitalism—or of sacrifices on the altar of human equality, grandiose ideals and high-sounding precepts—that's communism—or the most dangerous, middling notions of keeping peace with God and the Devil which are at bottom *hate* and jealousy and vainglory and the eternal drive to dominate and lord it over others and all the misery and pettiness that suffuse every human gesture no matter how small, and if I have taken the decision to write to you and use the address on your filthy and loathsome calling-card which is only another putrid expression of vanity and a twisted self-importance, it's because the deceased José appeared to me in a dream and pronounced your name and I recall that after saying *my poor brother Natán* he added *He has so much to learn,* as he was walking pensively along the river-bank or seashore or lakeshore he turned back to me and said, *My poor brother Natán, he has so much to learn* and I couldn't answer him because I was as if paralyzed, but if he were now to appear before me, and I wish he would, I would tell him what the man they call Jesus is supposed to have said: *Give not that which is holy unto the dogs, neither cast ye your pearls before swine, lest they trample them under their feet, and turn again and rend you.*

I have to finish with this letter because the nurse, *accursed one,* has come to give me my injection.

> Yours sincerely,
> Gabriel Perdomo

The second letter, which Natán found slid under his door, was from Teresa.

Dear Natán,

By the time you see these lines, I will no longer be your neighbor. Felipe, the girls and I are moving out today.

I'm not giving you the new address or phone number because even if it pains me to leave this way, and I might suffer for a short time afterward, I've decided I can't see you any more.

I didn't want to say anything because I didn't want to cause you any worry, but Felipe suspects I'm seeing another man, I know he has no proof but he seems to have noticed a change in me and when he presses me to make love with him he asks me through the whole thing if I care for him and if I'm doing it with someone else too, and he calls me dishonest and frigid and once after finishing he spat on me and called me a slut and even slapped me, although fortunately he didn't go beyond that.

Two nights ago he went over the same litany and made me swear on my mother's life that I wasn't in love with someone else and I swore on my mother's life. Then he told me to swear on my father's grave and I swore on my father's grave. Then he made me kneel at the bedside and told me, Swear on your two daughters, and I swore on my two daughters. May your daughters fall ill; may my daughters fall ill. May your daughters die at once; may my daughters die at once—and all the time looking me straight in the eye, so I couldn't avert my gaze.

Natán, I cannot go on this way. I have loved you deeply but I cannot leave Felipe because he's the father of my children and despite his drunken spells and the fact that he's almost illiterate, to the point that in his whole life I think he hasn't read a single book, he's a decent husband and a good father. I met him in Spain at a very sad moment of my life and he was alone and hardly drank at all, and we married and came to the United States to find a better life because part of my family was here, but he has no one here and this would fall very hard on him because he would have to go back to Spain and leave his daughters whom he loves so much. In other words, I don't have the strength to leave him.

My daughters love him, and even if they have liked you the few times they've seen you, it's not the same thing.

Anyway, you've never asked me to divorce, nor have you told me that you would take care of them if I should part from Felipe, and I'm not in a position to ask you for anything because we've been together with no obligations on either side. And for another thing I've seen that you're a man who basically prefers to be alone and my girls and I would only wind up being a drag on you.

I have no regrets about what's passed between us, I've had some very happy moments and I'll never forget the time in that restaurant when you told me how much you liked the way I was. But at the same time I can see I've become vile and I feel so low, the lowest of women. Every time I kiss and hug my daughters I watch myself defiling them, and it's the most horrible thing I've felt in my life.

On top of all that, I can sense that someone is following me, stalking me, and please don't think I'm imagining things. Three or four times, in different places, I've seen a man in a hat watching me from a distance. I've come to the conclusion that Felipe is paying him to spy on me.

The last night you and I were together, when I left for my mom's house to pick up my girls, he was leaning on a tree right near the building, he was there in spite of the rain and I could feel him smiling when he saw me go by.

That's why I told Felipe I wanted to move when the lease was up, and he, who says he's never much liked the place because it's far out of the way, was downright happy to hear it.

I beg you not to come looking for me. Please forget about me. You're still a young man and smart, and you won't be lacking for women.

I wish you the best of everything.

—T.

CHAPTER
NINE

"The doctor is in a consultation and can't see you before eleven. You can wait here, or you're welcome to wait in the garden. If you haven't had breakfast, there's a cafeteria at the end of this hallway. It's good, and it's reasonable."

"Thank you."

"What do you think about our boys in the Gulf? Pretty terrific, aren't they?"

"Absolutely."

"I hope the doctor lets you see your friend. I would like to help, but we have to go by the rules. The visits are all supervised, for the sake of the patients. Too bad you didn't call first. It's a long way from Miami."

"I like driving. Anyway, it's a beautiful morning. I think I'll walk outside for a bit. By the way—did you ever know a fellow called Tim Harris?"

"Tim Harris? I don't think so. Why?"

"No reason—just a thought I had. I'll take a walk in the garden and then I might stop by the cafeteria."

"Tell me if you need anything. As soon as I'm able to speak with the doctor, I'll let you know."

Natán beat a retreat from that woman whose affability he had at once mistrusted. Her well-played smile seemed to conceal a deeper purpose. Her face reminded him of someone—not of a woman but of a young man he'd met while working in a department store after reaching exile and who, Natán later heard, had killed himself by cutting open his veins. Now, he imagined that the story of Tim's death might have been spread by Tim himself, in order to conceal his transformation into a woman. The nurse had clear masculine features; her eyes, nose and eyebrows were exactly Tim's, while her mouth was a little smaller. Natán could picture the fellow perfectly. His memory could reproduce people and places with photographic precision, and in recent days he had been playing with the idea that most of the people who crossed his path were actually from other periods of his life. They had returned to him, some in quite different shapes and others nearly identical. Even if they had new names and gestures, a certain something in these strangers led him to feel an undeniable familiarity.

He went out to the garden, which was more like the edge of a country field, dense and rippling with nature; but the field was broken by a tall iron fence, rising up from the lawn in a way that unmistakably showed the limits of free movement. Narrow pathways lined with colorful plants crisscrossed each other labyrinth-style around the hospital, which Tim Harris's lookalike had insisted on calling a convalescent home.

On the wide porch, empty rocking chairs were swaying mysteriously back and forth; and since the vague breeze was not nearly heady enough to move them, one was led to suspect the presence of invisible forces.

Even so, it was a beautiful morning; Natán had not misspoken there. The carefully cut grass was wet from a rain that had excited an intense fragrance from the ground—an aroma that seemed to rise from the entrails of the garden, where the staff, or so Natán thought, might have buried disobedient patients—where Gabriel Perdomo, whom he had come to see, might also wind up, if indeed he was not already there.

Natán took a seat on a swing under a tree. Beyond the iron bars, abundant rows of orange trees were stretching nearly to the ocean. The morning air, full of sea-salt, struck his face with a crystalline coolness. The land around him seemed to be submerged in a transparent sea. In the distance, a boat was moving away on a striking blue surface that, instead of water, looked like a newly finished painting. Surely, on that boat, happy people were traveling to unknown lands, ignorant of dangers that would soon put an end to their fatal innocence. He checked an impulse to swing himself into the tree. For three days he had had no sleep.

At the side of the building rose a decrepit, knotted oak tree that was out of place amid the sparkling vegetation and immaculate white walls, instead reminding Natán of a dried-up tree in the yard at a house he'd inhabited during boyhood—a tree that for many months had been the subject of an argument between his parents, who seemed relieved to find something outside themselves onto which they could pour their unhappiness. His mother spoke of the tree with hatred, calling it useless and painful to the eye; while his father, implacably annoyed at this devout woman he badly wanted to leave, stubbornly defended it. A hurricane resolved their dispute; in a deluge that kept up for a week, the tree gave up before the relentless attack of wind and water. With a huge racket, its heavy branches collapsed onto the chicken-coop; an army of ants occupied the dismembered trunk; and among the ravaged, wasted roots, a snake built its nest.

As a child Natán had felt a close affinity with plants; he considered them secretly related to people, and his parents' argument over the tree appeared to confirm his suspicions. At the time, he was seven years old. Following one more in a series of moves instigated by his restless father, who was still gathering the nerve to break the chains of his familial confinement, his parents came face to face, in a new yard, with another weathered and wounded old tree. This time, however, no argument took place, for in exchanges whose vileness Natán remembered clearly after three decades, his parents resolved to separate; and the boy and his mother would not have to witness another tree's destruction, because they went to live at grandma's house before the next hurricane season began.

When he reached his teens, Natán forgot about his love of vegetation; his curiosity about humans blocked out his wonder at plant-life. Now, in a country he couldn't quite call his own, lacking any family, lacking even a lover, and bombarded by uncertainties about the existence or nonexistence of his half-brother, he felt his old, ardent desire to investigate the secret lives of grass, flowers and trees.

Sitting on the swing as he waited for Gabriel Perdomo's doctor to allow or disallow his visit, Natán occupied his mind in pulling at the skein of circumstances that had brought him to this place, the west coast of Florida near the town of Naples. His thoughts went here and there—from his father's letter mentioning a certain José Velázquez, which had started him on the search, then back to inchoate memories of his Cuban childhood, then abruptly to episodes of his adolescence and adulthood—every scene or detail or story having a subtle, arcane connection to every other.

Remembering the voice of the woman who had called in the middle of the night to give him the address where someone by his brother's name was working as a night-watchman, he seemed to recognize the timbre of his first girlfriend, three years older than himself, who after a brief pursuit had given herself to him—in a standing position, behind the wall of a church in ruins. The place had been of her choosing. Later, he found out that the girl had performed the same act with other youngsters of the neighborhood, in the same spot. Natán could not remember her face; but his awakening memory, as if pushed along by a light wind, dredged up the image of a bell-shaped skirt and the echo of a girl's voice whispering falsehoods of love by the wall, in the very tone of the stranger who said on the phone: "You left a message for José Velázquez?"

The mysterious car that had tailed him from Alicia Lastre's house, on that first visit, took shape as the one he had totaled right after his arrival in the United States—an accident that had nearly cost him his life. People, places, objects, trees and animals intertwined to form a closely knit web around him.

Just then, a group of some ten men and women came out of a pavilion at the far side of the garden and went toward the entrance of the main building. All of them were smoking with gusto, as if they were inhaling not smoke but oxygen in a place where the air is thin. They did not speak among themselves; they were slow and slovenly, moving with erratic steps; those who didn't hold their heads low seemed to be looking carefully at some vague point on the horizon, or to be seeing something so indefinite it couldn't possibly exist; and their silence conferred on them a misleading air of calm—except for an old guy muttering something between his teeth, overcome by an infantile wrath.

Natán didn't know any of them, but somehow their faces were

familiar: they were the same faces he had seen in the small, jam-packed waiting rooms of seers, astrologers and *santeros;* the same people who hung around in those stores called *botánicas* where you could find potions to make you forget betrayals and failures, elixirs to sway lovers, prayers to banish harmful spirits, amulets for the helpless—the ones Natán had called *faces of loneliness.*

Here they were again, in this lunatic asylum that went by the name of "convalescent home" on the outskirts of Naples, ensconced among flowers, orange trees and meadows very near the sea, where a ship slowly traversing the waters was a tiny vignette in the explosion of blue.

Here they were, without their bearings on a tranquil day, carrying with a rather grim gentleness the shame of knowing they were different.

A youngster broke off from the group and came toward Natán. His frisky, clownlike step shook his ample blond hair as though it were a wig placed casually on his head, but otherwise exquisite. He wore golden rings in the lobes and upper parts of his ears, as well as a shiny small ring inlaid in his nose. A slender mustache emphasized the thickness of his lips. After a timid, roundabout approach, the boy stopped in front of Natán and with flatly inexpressive eyes he said: "Excuse me, sir. Do you need a slave?"

Natán, embarrassed, stood up from the swing and wiped some nonexistent spots off his pants. "No."

"Are you sure, sir? I would like to be your slave. I'm ready to do whatever you tell me. I need money."

The youngster, no more than twenty, gripped his own throat as he talked, and for a second Natán thought he was being playful; but the boy's well-proportioned face was quite serious, and in his vacant stare there appeared no hint of humor.

"No, I don't need a slave," Natán said firmly.

"But sir, I'll be a good slave. I'll be whatever you tell me to be. I need money."

"Money for what?"

"For many things, sir, for many things."

With his melodious voice, it sounded like a musical refrain.

"What things?"

"Drugs, sir. I need to get high."

"I can't give you money, certainly not for drugs. Anyway, you won't be finding any drugs in this place. Do you know a man by the name of Gabriel?"

"You mean Gabriel the angel?"

"Gabriel the Cuban-American. He's been admitted here."

"Maybe, maybe not. I know an angel called Gabriel. He appeared before the Virgin Mary, and he will blow the trumpet on Judgment Day."

Natán took two steps back.

"We are not speaking about the same person."

"I need money, sir. I'm ready to show you something—something that will impress you."

The boy moved his face brazenly close to Natán's, as if to kiss him. He had menthol on his breath. Natán was afraid the boy might pounce on him or do something obscene, and start a scandal in the middle of that manicured garden where he himself, though only a visitor, could be accused of indecent behavior.

"You're quite mistaken," Natán told the boy. "I am not a pervert."

"We are all that, sir," the boy said with conviction, and eyes that were abysmally cold.

"Yes, you're right, but perversion has many forms—and within limits, within limits."

"Sir, I have no limits. Look and see."

Natán was about to turn away and take his distance in order to avoid a fight with the boy who, along with his drug addiction, was clearly a prostitute; but the boy, instead of exposing his private parts as Natán had feared, showed a pair of wrists graven with deep scars.

"Razor blades, six months ago. Give me three dollars for each."

Natán pulled out his wallet and with a trembling hand produced a ten-dollar bill. The boy snatched the money and started rolling up his shirt.

"Let me show you this other one, sir. This was my father's penknife; it didn't have such a sharp edge."

"I don't want to see it—I don't want to see it."

"A dollar for this one, sir. Come on, just a dollar more. It's not as deep."

From out of nowhere appeared a middle-aged woman with a paper crown on her head. She gave the boy a good hard slap, and for the first time his face had a human aspect.

"On your knees!" the woman shouted at him. "On your knees, before your Majesty! That's it, on your knees, without moving! Don't get up until I order you!" Turning to Natán, she pronounced in a thick British accent: "I do beg your pardon, my good man, if this miserable child has troubled you. He's lowborn, a scoundrel, completely unlettered. Please state your grievances and I will have him flogged; or if you wish it, I will flog him myself, this very moment, before your eyes."

"No, that won't be necessary," Natán said with chagrin as he looked at the young man on his knees, gazing up at the woman with wonder.

"But didn't he trouble you?" the woman addressed Natán with scorn. "I cannot permit my servants to frighten emissaries from other kingdoms. You are an emissary, are you not? An emissary, or perhaps a spy. The world is quite full of those. With whom do I have the pleasure of speaking?"

"My name is Natán. In English that would be Nathan."

"A Jew, are you not?"

"Cuban."

The woman reached into the space between her breasts and pulled out an old coin with a Latin inscription in a quadrilateral.

"Are you acquainted with that symbol?"

"I'm afraid not."

The woman brought her gaze close to Natán's and said defiantly: "Do not prevaricate, sir!"

"I assure you, I have no reason to lie."

The kneeling boy let loose with crackling snarls, like an irascible dog. Despite the morning coolness, Natán had broken into a sweat. The woman, after a good long look into his eyes, gave a gesture of disdain and averted herself. Then she turned back to tell him: "You cannot deceive me. I am aware of who sent you. Now, tell me the whole truth."

"Tell her the truth," the boy chimed in.

"Silence!" the woman shouted and gave the boy's head a resounding crack. "Who is it, then, who feeds you?"

"It is you, your Majesty," the boy said in a whisper.

"Who gives you protection from your enemies?" she said, striking the boy's head once again.

"You, your Majesty."

"And who is it who pulled you out of the mud?"

"You, your Majesty."

Some of the other patients, crossing the garden, looked on with indifference; or at least their eyes were turned in that direction, even as their neutral expressions made one wonder if they realized what was going on, absorbed as they seemed to be in their private, solitary dreams. Natán was about to tell the woman to leave the youngster in peace when a nurse came along, treading firmly on the gravel path.

"Shirley! Mark! That's enough!"

With a somber dignity, the lady reached down to the damp lawn and picked up the paper crown that had fallen when she had so forcibly struck the boy. The lad got to his feet in a hurry, brushed off his clothes and ran away groaning.

"Shirley, please go to your room!" commanded the nurse who looked like Tim Harris. Turning to Natán, she said: "I'm sorry, but the doctor won't be able to see you for two hours."

"I'll have a look around Naples and come back," answered Natán, eager to escape the garden as quickly as he could.

Within half an hour Natán was roaming the beach that skirted the city, strewn with an enormous variety of shells that suggested the scraps of a life turned to residue—singular, even beautiful, but residue all the same. On this winter morning, the broad fringe of sand was deserted. Homes along the beach, obscured by walls or fences, studded with signs declaiming "Private Property" and "Keep Off," gave a like impression of being uninhabited. Only the birds teeming in branches, or pelicans afloat on the sea, recalled the world of living beings, different in their restlessness from the immobile but ever-watchful trees. He sat down on the edge of a dock to observe the constant motion of waves crashing into the pilings. He felt steeped in the loneliness of the place, in the immensity of sea and sky.

Vainly, in these immaculate surroundings, did he search for a human figure—just as, during the past week, he had vainly sought for any presence or trace of the man or spirit or ghost that had been hounding him ever since his visit to the lamented Alicia. Her voice did not resound in his mind—the silence only deepened his

CARLOS VICTORIA

memory—and in the photo he saw the lady by herself, seated on
her favorite chair, without a trace or smudge or spot of any kind in
the place where the stranger, a replica of Natán's father, had once
appeared reflectively to scrutinize the lens.

Pretending the photo was a thing he had found by chance in
the street, Natán had showed the picture to his boss—who grudg-
ingly gave him two more weeks off—to neighbors, to co-workers,
and then to anyone who crossed his path, but no one who looked
at it could see the man; they only saw old Alicia, whose ironic
expression never faded.

Vainly, too, had he sat on his balcony, hour after hour, with the
volume of Keats open on his knees, gazing at the forest, at the
water's rough edge, at the rundown docks where crewless boats
were bobbing; and he looked farther away, at the gigantic runway
where military planes landed with a heavy roar, or at a distant shore-
line where squatters, empty of means but full of audacity, had ille-
gally occupied pieces of land and built makeshift houses that were
an eyesore in the luxuriant landscape. Vainly had he traversed those
places where the stranger had let himself be seen: the environs of
Alicia Lastre's old house, the cemetery that housed his mother's
remains, the corner near the naked ladies' bar, even the apartment
complex in Miami Lakes where he had found the Keats poem. The
person or apparition had vanished without leaving the smallest
clue.

And Teresa—the only one to perceive the white-haired head in
that photo disfigured by the sweat of many hands or by continuous travel in tight pockets—even Teresa, by her own word, had
taken herself away for good.

Natán bore her no ill will. Indeed, with the passage of days he
found out, bit by bit, how much he cared for her. Phrases or gestures that once had seemed insignificant now claimed a broader

place in his memory; words thrown out by chance echoed for hours with the resonance of his affection. He had chosen to respect the decision she'd made as a wife, as a mother, as a woman swayed by duty, love, honor, fear, or whatever other motive; so he had not gone looking for her. Still, in the course of the task he had set himself of finding his brother—was that it, really?—he secretly hoped to see her if only from a distance, in the company of her two little girls, or coming out of a clothing store with her melancholy, self-critical gait.

Miami, however, had thousands of streets, dozens of neighborhoods; the squat architecture, fit for people who have spent their lives on the move, going from one place to another, fleeing governments or prisons or stifling miseries or perhaps themselves, reached for untold miles from the sea to the edges of deserted swamps; and years could go by before Lady Luck might grant him the pleasure of meeting her.

In the silence of this empty beach, treading on the infinite variety of shells, with only seabirds and coastal vegetation for company, with every particle around him seeming to radiate calm, Natán had the abrupt impression of being in the midst of an uproar, in the eye of a storm.

He couldn't release from his mind a set of recurring ideas: that this tranquil sand and sea, this quiet, gleaming horizon, held in its innards the remains of thousands who had disappeared, the victims of plots and lies, of deadly games that had started out as innocent, simple pastimes; that beings or objects, even after perishing, came to life in other forms; and that the subtle connection he'd discovered between his past and his present, involving people, animals, trees and lifeless objects, was nothing more or less than the fact of destruction itself.

This process of transformation—one of the mainstays of

modern science, which at other times he had studied through reading—now showed itself to him for the first time in its destructive guise; and he recognized it like a message written in an unknown alphabet that one comes to understand as fully as a phrase in one's mother tongue. Having perceived the devastation, he was at a loss as to how he could survive on this minefield.

Perhaps, he thought, a brother's advice might help him through this labyrinth of destruction; but his brother had declined to show up. And Natán was alone, quite alone, in this place that had somehow turned out to be a replica of beaches in Cuba; maybe the beach to the south of Camagüey where he had spent time as a teenager with his father—only on that occasion, his own youth, as well as the stifling company of his elder, had not let him perceive the winds of desolation encircling that perfectly quiet, beautiful, isolated spot. Natán and his father had fished from sunrise to sunset, and even had some luck. They had gotten a one-hundred-pound marlin, as well as mountains of snapper and shad whose bones later blackened in the frying pan where lard bubbled without a stop. The skin on their hands had been cracked by sun, rock salt, and the treacherous points of fish hooks. The conversation between them, in line with custom, was kept to the simplest things. The silences at last became insufferable to the boy, who yearned for more than fishing lessons. And the bright light of midday was harshness itself.

His visit to Gabriel, whose letter had made a strong impression, was a quest for a guiding thread that might rescue him, not from death and transfiguration—the inescapable destiny he could learn to accept—but from the isolation growing in him since the departure of Teresa and of that real or imagined being who, despite the terror he struck, had also become a part of his life.

Natán knew he should be glad for the culmination he himself

had wished: never again to see that shadow whose purposes he could not understand; never again to hear the footfall or voice or breathing of that person or object or insistent fantasy; but like the bored lover who disdains his partner's company until the partner goes away, he longed for the terror that the stranger's presence had roused in him.

At the two-hour mark, Natán was back at the hospital. He followed the instructions of a receptionist, who told him the doctor was waiting for him and showed him to the consulting room; but as he passed through the long corridor and came upon the statue of a rider straining to control a wild horse, he wavered and realized he had forgotten what to say. Indeed, he reflected, his visit was as out of place as that horseman wrought in metal; but at last he knocked on the appointed door.

The doctor's office was a narrow cubicle that could hardly contain a desk and two chairs; no paintings, curtains, books or windows were there to offer a lull from the violent intimacy that forced itself on two people who had never seen each other before.

Natán was surprised to find the other fellow—whom he'd imagined to be a typical American, tall, blond and blue-eyed—so tiny that one could consider him a dwarf, with sallow skin and dark hair. His English, though quite correct, revealed a foreign background that Natán, fairly expert in such matters, could not pinpoint.

The eyes were most disturbing of all. The left one, a depthless green, looked empty of life, while the right, shiny black, had a peculiar sparkle that seemed intent on compensating for the dullness of the other.

Natán couldn't help thinking about the eyes of the seer David, which worked a similar kind of fascination, as if their deformity conferred a kind of hypnotic power. It then struck Natán that this interview was another in a string of the consultations he'd held during the past month with people who claimed to be interpreters in the language of cards, hand-lines, stars, waking spirits, stones, shells, saints or crystal balls; and that more than being simply a psychiatrist who's available to inform a visitor about the case of a patient in strict isolation—the nurse had told Natán that Gabriel was in a solitary room, for reasons of security—this individual, perhaps a native of Saudi Arabia or India or North Africa, was about to reveal a secret of Natán's own past, present or future.

"What's your relation to the patient?" the doctor asked after introducing himself with a few pleasantries; the man's Anglo-Saxon name, Walter Sheridan, was baffling.

"I scarcely know him," Natán confessed.

"I see," the doctor said, leaning forward as if to scrutinize the visitor's blushing face. The black eye, blinking lightly, seemed to take in more life.

"It's a very long and complicated story," Natán said sheepishly, much as he'd resolved not to be cowed by the other's intense gaze. "I know you have more than enough to do, and I don't want to waste your time."

"We have all the time in the world," the doctor said quite sternly.

"This is rather personal. In brief, Gabriel Perdomo is a friend of my brother's—my half-brother, whom I've been trying to locate for quite some time—and I think he can give me a clue, an idea of how to find him. Do you think I might see him for a short visit, perhaps ten minutes? I promise I won't take more time."

Walter Sheridan was silent. *He's an actor,* Natán thought. *He wants to intimidate me, show his authority.*

Finally the doctor said: "Gabriel is in no condition to receive visitors. He's going through an aggressive stage, which makes him dangerous to himself and to others, and we have to keep him in physical restraints. He's strapped to his bed, and we're obliged to keep him under sedation. I don't think he can give you any information about your half-brother. Gabriel has had no contact with reality for some time. He's over the edge, as we say—entirely under the influence of delusions from his illness. He probably doesn't even remember who your brother is."

"But he wrote to me just a short time ago."

"Gabriel, or your brother?"

"Gabriel. Of course it's the letter of someone in a crisis, but I wouldn't call it completely divorced from reality. It mentions my half-brother several times, and it's one of the reasons I came here."

"Can you show it to me?"

"I didn't bring it."

"It's true he has his lucid moments, and I'm using the word indulgently, but those moments are so ephemeral they don't offer much hope. The brother you mention—what's his relation to him?"

"They seem to be good friends."

"For how long?"

"I'm not sure—maybe a few years. I think they knew each other before Gabriel got sick, or at any rate before his condition worsened. They saw each other often and spoke a lot. After all, they're both Cuban—though that might not be so important."

"Where did they meet, here or there?"

"I don't know."

"What does your brother do?"

"My brother? It's hard to say. He's always been a bit unstable. He likes to travel and enjoy himself."

"Travel, enjoy himself ..." the doctor mumbled. "Maybe he also likes drugs?"

"My brother? I don't think so. And I'm not sure the question is proper. It seems rather off-putting, actually—more like a policeman's question than a psychiatrist's."

The doctor smiled, and his good eye shone with pleasure. Natán felt as if the office had suddenly become a cage.

"Excuse me," Walter Sheridan said. "The patients in this convalescent home have a peculiar problem of which you might not be aware: they have all committed crimes that stem from their mental troubles. This is not exactly what you would call a criminal institution, but we are not so far from that. We work with the authorities, even as a private institution—and that's beneficial for those who would otherwise be living in much less agreeable conditions. In other words, our clients are from families who can support their stay with us; because, to speak frankly, this isn't free, and they are here because the law put them here. Gabriel Perdomo's case is a particularly troubling one. For years he abused drugs—cocaine, heroine, finally crack—which intensified a mental condition he has suffered since his adolescent years. He claims to be part of a band of assassins about which he doesn't want to say anything specific, and which is certainly a product of fantasy. What is true is that he has committed violence against family members and others close to him; and I am talking about real violence which on at least three occasions made necessary the hospitalization of his victims, who didn't want to make complaints to the police. Finally, his violence almost caused the death of an innocent bystander completely unrelated to him. That was the decisive factor in his coming here. Have no doubts: we are dealing with a dangerous man."

As he spoke, the doctor opened and closed his hands on the bare desktop; and Natán could see it was not only the man's eyes that were different from each other. His right hand was pale and thin, as if about to dry up, while the left was chubby and greenish-yellow in color.

"When I saw him in the Miami hospital, he didn't seem violent," Natán said as he tried to keep from looking at the other man's eyes or hands, fixing his gaze on the medallion hanging from the doctor's neck, rather similar to the ornament on the woman patient who thought she was a queen. "To be sure, he seemed unbalanced, but he also showed a quite extraordinary culture and intelligence. He didn't give the impression of being a criminal."

"Yes, Gabriel is smart and well educated. And no one is saying he's a common criminal; but we also know he moved in a sordid circle of drug-users and dealers, who might have taken advantage of him because he had a lot of money from his family—a family that treated him irresponsibly, with an overindulgent love, as is often the case, and in order to keep him quiet they didn't refuse him anything, which only hastened his decline. That's why I asked you about your brother. The people who called themselves Gabriel's friends were of the worst caliber, as far as I can tell. And as a specialist with access to his history, I know plenty."

Natán waved his hand back and forth across his face, as if the doctor's breath had sullied him.

"I'm sure my brother is not one of those people. Quite the opposite: Gabriel himself told me my brother has always tried to help him, that he's a man for whom money means nothing, that when he gets it he gives it away to others, that he's always treated Gabriel tenderly and thoughtfully, and that, indeed, my brother is almost a saint."

"You ought to know, better than I, who your brother is. What surprises me is that you don't know where he is, and you think Gabriel can help you."

"Well, the thing is, as I told you, we're only half-brothers, we've had problems in our family, and my half-brother wound up with the short end of the stick. Not even my mother knew of his existence. My father was, well, a little footloose—do you see?"

"I do. And when was the last time you saw your brother, or half-brother?"

"The last time? I think it must have been three weeks ago. No, two. I thought I saw him but I wasn't sure. It was from afar—he was on the other side of a lake—because I live next to a lake. And he was walking on the opposite shore. He goes there often, it's one of his favorite places."

"Does he also live near there?"

"I don't know where he lives. Otherwise I wouldn't have come here. In fact I know very little about him. Some people have given me pieces of information. I used to have a photo ..."

Natán fell silent. He felt exposed, humiliated, almost in tears. The doctor's unequal eyes were scrutinizing him with a brash impertinence.

At last Sheridan said: "Mr. Velázquez, rather than seeing Gabriel Perdomo I think you should go for professional help. I'm a psychiatrist. I give professional help and I can see you need it. Do you have medical insurance?"

Natán, reddening, got to his feet. "Doctor, that is offensive. If you are telling me I'm crazy ..."

"No one has used that word."

"Well, it's obvious you're thinking it."

"What's obvious, Mr. Velázquez, is that your emotional state leaves a lot to be desired. Please excuse my frankness. Your hands are shaking. Your tear-glands are ready to burst because you do not allow them to secrete their fluids, which could give you some relief, by the way. Your complexion is undergoing sudden changes, and your manner of sweating shows that you are close to a nervous collapse. Tell me: do you often take a drink?"

"Look here! I am not your patient."

"You should be. Your mouth is parched, and your saliva has turned to paste."

"That is ridiculous. May I see Gabriel Perdomo or not?"

"You can see him on the other side of a glass, if you wish. I warn you, it's not a pleasant sight. Come with me."

After passing in silence through a labyrinth of polished corridors—long lines of closed doors from behind which one could vaguely hear laughter, moans, coughing, murmuring and, at more than one door, screams—the small, nearly midget-sized doctor taking the lead with his rapid and light-footed step, like a wild animal on his toes, Natán lagging behind, exhausted by his long walk in the sand and two sleepless nights, trying to distract himself by glancing at the dull artworks—seascapes, still-lifes, pastoral scenes rendered with a lukewarm feeling, as empty and indifferent as the walls they inhabited, as far as could be from life's intensity—they finally went outside to a courtyard where patients were taking sun in deck chairs or just wandering about with absent expressions. In afternoon's full brightness, the feebleness of their faces and bodies looked indecently exposed, to the point where Natán thought these people would better be kept in a place with less light. At the end of the patio a corpulent man—self-assured in the raw physical power that was highlighted by his male nurse's uniform—got up from a chair near an iron door and greeted Sheridan.

"Greg, please open up, I want to see one of the children," the doctor said. "How have they been today?"

"Everything under control," the man pronounced in a strong Southern accent.

"Gabriel causing no more problems?"

"He's sleeping. They're all asleep."

Natán was piqued by the doctor's use of the word 'children' to refer to Gabriel and other patients in his condition, but held his tongue; he had resolved to keep his exchanges with this man to an absolute minimum. The nurse used a key to open the iron door and then a barred one that led to a narrow corridor lined by other doors, each with a rectangular glass window reinforced by iron bars. Natán shuddered at recalling Cuba's jails, in which he had spent time as a 'guest.'

"Gabriel is in number fifteen, right?" the doctor asked the nurse.

"Yes, in fifteen."

Sheridan showed Natán to one of the doors.

With a queasy feeling, Natán went up to the little window.

An aged man bound to the bed with leather straps, his face grimy, his hair disheveled, the whites of his eyes peeking out from behind half-closed eyelids, his mouth ringed with grit, was sleeping beneath a lamp's whitish light. Natán could hardly bring himself to believe that this wreck of a human, so roughly tied down, was the same person whose acquaintance he had made only months earlier. His features bore only a slight resemblance to the ones Natán remembered. No doubt, however, this was Gabriel—the only one in the world who could say whether José Velázquez was dead or alive; the only one who could talk about his half-brother's recent life; the only one who had been able, through the mysterious power of dreams, to visualize José at that lakeside, a place to which he had wandered out of worry over Natán and his lot. *My poor brother Natán,* José had said to this man who was now an empty vessel, subject to the whims of madness and a target for abuse by others. Could it be that, at this very moment, Gabriel dreamt of the same man Natán was seeking?

"If you could wake him for a moment," Natán said to the doctor, who was also peeping through the glass. "I just need a few minutes with him, to ask a couple of questions."

Sheridan put his motley hands together and cracked his fingers. "You really are quite something," he said. "Do you not see the patient's conditon?"

"You mean the prisoner's," Natán murmured.

"Would you rather he roamed free, assaulting people at random, threatening the lives of others who have no hand in his illness?"

When they went back out onto the patio, Natán told the doctor in an uncertain voice: "I see your point of view, and I'm grateful for the time you gave me. If you come to Miami you're welcome to call me. Here's my card."

The man's eyes had undergone a slight transformation. The dark one had retreated to a certain density, while the green eye, though still inert, was flashing like crystal in the sun.

"I would like to help you more, but you won't allow that."

"You can help me," Natán said after a brief silence. "You can help by telling me if in Gabriel Perdomo's file there appears a certain name, whether mentioned by him or uncovered during an investigation, since I have understood from what you said that an inquiry has been made concerning his case. Perhaps there might be some reference to my brother. I know this kind of information is confidential but perhaps an exception can be made, because what I'm looking for has no direct relation to Gabriel's case."

"I'm sorry, I cannot help you there. This is not a matter of breaching confidentiality, which I would be disposed to do, since this concerns a side-issue, and I can see it has a special importance for you. I myself, actually, have two siblings, a brother and a sister. But before you and I met today I reviewed Gabriel's record, since the lady nurse told me you wanted to see him, and I found nothing there about a particular friend, only the usual references to his family, and of course to his victims. All of them were women."

"But you spoke about evil companions."

"Unnamed individuals," the doctor said with some impatience. "The police investigators made note of them without using names. Gabriel's relatives mention them too, and as usual they blame them for everything. But there's nothing specific. To tell you the truth, I reviewed the file to see if your name was there, but it wasn't. Not yours, nor that of any friend. And likewise, in the sessions with me Gabriel made no specific reference to anyone. He's not communicative in matters regarding his personal life. Besides, the world he inhabits is a world of death and grief, like that of most people with mental illness. In that way he's just like the rest. It's one of the fingerprints of madness."

"Do you think so?"

"I don't think, I know," the doctor said, extending his crippled hand. Natán, on shaking it, was taken aback by the touch of its notably cold skin.

"Excuse me if I spoke rather roughly," Natán said while avoiding the other man's disturbing gaze, which had come back to scrutinize him with a relentless curiosity.

"Never mind. But I reiterate my suggestion that you find some kind of therapeutic help. You can be well looked-after here. I also have a private practice. It all depends on whether you have insurance, as I imagine you do. I like to call things as I see them, and I see you are suffering from a marked nervous disorder that will greatly worsen with time. You can still head it off."

"I'll give it some thought."

"Very good. I must leave you now, I'm awaited elsewhere. If you follow this corridor without making any turns, you'll find the exit."

Natán hurried out of the building, steering clear of nurses and staff. Outside, the garden still had its fragrance of moistened earth.

At the parking lot on the hospital's outskirts, he paused to listen to a song in Spanish that was coming from a nearby bar, a ballad he hadn't heard since childhood. A woman's anguished voice was accompanied by the monotone of a guitar that was also full of feeling. He recalled having heard his mother sing that ballad, before she gave up the vanities of this world to embrace a more stable God. He broke into sobs, just for a moment, then got in the car. It surprised him; he couldn't remember having cried in years.

At dusk, after stopping at an auto mechanic's—his motor oil had been dripping like sweat from a human body, making a puddle on the asphalt, and luckily the red warning light had lit up on the dashboard before he started his return trip—Natán took off from Naples.

Obviously the trip had been useless; or so he thought as he drove by the city's last suburbs. All he had learned was that Gabriel's companions, before he entered the asylums, had been delinquents and drug addicts, which in some way led him to suspect that José Velázquez had been part of a corrupt and lawless environment.

He thought back to those confusing statements by Gladys, José's hairdresser girlfriend, which had left Natán wondering whether his brother might have been, among other things, a criminal. His ex-lover Mercedes, on the other hand, had insisted, like Alicia and Gabriel himself, that José possessed a generous and loving nature. Anyway, Natán reflected, the one did not exclude the other. His car sped up on the empty highway, leaving farther and farther behind all traces of city life. Criminals there are, he told himself, who despite their ugly deeds can act kindheartedly—except of course to their victims. At that moment he entered the gloomy precincts of the Everglades marshes. Dark clouds were lazily scattering across a taciturn sky.

Nor could he trust the psychiatrist. That person of unclear ethnicity with disturbing eyes, who seemed more interested in getting clients than in being of help to another human being, gave him the willies. Natán found striking the doctor's statement that the world of the mentally ill was "a world of death and grief"—as if he had guessed the very thoughts that had come to haunt Natán, and indeed as if he were accusing him of being in a deep mental crisis, as a way of underlining his invitation that Natán place himself in treatment.

Natán recognized he was not in a normal frame of mind; but he could not accept that the causes of his imbalance were to be found in his brain, still less that they could be remedied with medications, electric shock or lengthy therapy.

No, his present affliction lay in his loneliness, lack of knowledge, lack of a handle on things; above all in his uncertainty about the intentions of the mysterious figure that prowled in unforeseen places; and then, by extension, in his uncertainty about the intentions of others, of acquaintances or strangers or—why deny it—supernatural beings.

Now, on this abandoned road that traversed the endless mud flats, with lines of thin vegetation broken in places by distressed little woods, Natán felt an obligation to pause and consider his old friends, or perhaps his enemies, the trees. He paid no heed to the wastelands of grass and stagnant water, nor to the forbidding patches of lowland crisscrossed by canals that circulated through underbrush parched by the cold, like veins running through a lifeless body; but rather he observed the woodlands, the families of shrubs that had gathered as if to hatch a conspiracy, the pines and eucalyptus trees that protruded defiantly at the edges of the asphalt strip.

The trees bore him little comfort in the chilly dusk of March.

The cedars now splayed in the mud might have given him guidance when they were growing tall, but their splattered corpses only called to mind the utter barrenness of decease. It was, he thought, a cataleptic landscape, where all sense and motion were being arrested by the light that, in its gradual dissolution, erased forms and blurred colors. His foot, propelled by its own energy, pressed down on the accelerator, and at moments the car raced out of his control. The palpable sense of mortality rising from the ground was pushing him to speed up the journey.

Only the animals possessed a stubborn vitality. Flocks of birds went flying from one clump of trees to another, turning as precisely as acrobats, piercing into the tight density of branches to alight triumphantly on an open bough; rabbits leapt audaciously in the yellow grasslands; squirrels ran in jagged lines, hurrying up the trunks of pine trees right to their unsteady tops; insects were swarming in the air, smashing themselves to death against his windshield and hood; birds of prey, poised on telephone wires and poles, beat their ominous wings and embarked on short, pointless flights, perhaps to show the traveler, in their frank and ghastly way, that they were profiteers of death.

A sudden, reddish glow from the depths of a forest made him stop. A fire was devouring the vegetation. When he had pulled off the road and parked his car, he realized it was only tortured sunlight that had momentarily thrown off the steely cloud cover and was now invading the shadowy solitude of the pines, coloring their leaves and bark purple.

A figure with a terse and lively step was making its way through the close-woven foliage. Still in the car, Natán held his breath and scanned the brightly lit thicket. The silence broke when a fly came in through the window and hovered near his head. He was about to get moving again when a noise in the leaves held him back.

From among the reddened tree-trunks, delicate and still, a deer was watching. For a few tense moments, man and animal traded glances; but when Natán opened his door with the idea of approaching, the deer took off and vanished into the depths of the shining forest.

That brief apparition, ethereal presence and rapid flight made Natán even sadder, and he took up his journey more slowly, pausing to look at both sides of the road, trying to decipher the obtuse language of flora and fauna. Along the rough roadsides, from the flatland of weeds and water, stood forth white-colored trees whose trunks and branches appeared to have been drained of blood. Here and there, too, Natán found a trailer or a shack whose inhabitants, he supposed, were hermits disaffected by the so-called civilized world.

Night kept falling. Cars with headlights on, looking like giant insects, passed by his own along the narrow roadway, going by so fast he could not get a clear view of who was traveling in them. He would rather have liked to stop those cars and ask the drivers where they were going, or from where they had come; but no sooner had they appeared than they became indistinct spots in the rearview mirror, before fading completely away.

Without warning, the road became a bridge that carried him over sleeping lakes or islands crowded with vegetation. Nauseating fumes rose from stinking waters. At a railroad crossing a short distance from the highway, a man was leaning over the tracks as if to hammer the rails. Natán slowed down and looked at that face in the darkness, but the man's solitary attitude invited no conversation. The man did not even raise his head.

Farther on, the landscape grew even less hospitable. The trees dwindled to become curious markers, odd shapes that set off a faceless, monotonous terrain. Along with night came a chill, and frost glistened on withered leaves.

When daylight had fled, leaving a vague and filmy halo that was quickly absorbed by energetic clouds, Natán had the impression that just as night had fallen on the earth, enveloping it in lethal darkness, so had it descended on his own life; and he was being compelled to enter it as his car hurried along under a listless sky, eating mile after mile of this barren swamp, where the kingdom of shadows ruled supreme.

CHAPTER

TEN

Most disturbing of all was the odor. He couldn't tell whether it was coming from the bed-sheets, furniture, bathroom, kitchen shelves or balcony—or maybe it was something stuck to his nose, with no relation to outside objects or places. At times it was so vague as to be a mere suggestion, while at others it came in gusts.

When it started, he had expended some effort in trying to un-cover it. The smell was familiar, piercing, intoxicating; it evoked playgrounds, gardens, altars, humid crannies, country lanes—places where he had shed the smooth skin of infancy and grown the angst-ridden shell of a teenager. It seemed to him that he had also sensed it more recently, but he couldn't say exactly where, until one day, while he was waiting at a red light, when he saw a blind man cross the street with upright dignity, he remembered the seer David and realized that the odor haunting him night and day was the scent of basil.

He recalled a spinster aunt, a sister of his father's, who used to make secret visits to a place for séances—her brothers, on whom she materially depended, were all fanatical communists—grew basil in flower-pots near her window and took the herb, sprig after sprig, to the sessions where mediums brandished it with a great fuss to make evil spirits vanish.

Then and there Natán welcomed the fragrance as a good omen. The following day it disappeared, as if he only needed to consider it a protective shield for it to fade away.

Late at night, his neighbors far descended into the valley of sleep, some heavy footfalls in the corridor got him out of bed and moved him, wrapped in a bed-sheet, to look through his peephole at the concave space outside, waiting for the passerby to cross his field of vision. The footfalls disappeared into the stairwell. As soon as he returned to bed, they resumed as an echo. At instants they sounded on the roof. His sense of hearing had sharpened to the point where he could hear the repetitions of a melody that might be soothing an insomniac, the muffled weeping of a temperamental or hungry child, the rustling of water at the dock, the swarming of insects in the grass, the vibration of cars on the distant highway, and at moments, permeating the breeze that wafted among the huge, dark trees, a voice that whispered a single word, a familiar word, a name: *Natán.*

He went out on the balcony, shivering in the chill, ready to answer, to face the air that had been sullied by that call—for indeed someone had called him, or so he had felt on opening the glass door—but at that moment the air went silent and he, leaning on the balcony rail, was taken aback by the stillness around him; it was as if every living thing had paused in its most insignificant motion, or as if he had been struck deaf.

On an earlier occasion, he remembered, a woman's voice had pronounced from the shore: *He isn't here.* Then, from the airport, as if in response to the woman's incantation, had come the thunderous roar of a plane's engine, replenishing the sky with its familiar concert of sounds.

It was not just his senses of smell and hearing that played tricks on him, or perhaps disclosed to him a hidden reality; his sight seemed to be suffering from an unnatural intensification, as if distorted by a powerful drug, and he was able, at those trancelike instants, to look closely into the rugged surfaces of walls and find faces, hidden landscapes, unclear markings, clumps of vegetation, maps or sketches in the rough cement, as they might appear under a microscope's lens; or when he looked at the wood across the lake, he could focus with an abrupt clarity on leaves or roots, could tell one tree from another, one branch from another, and precisely judge, with a bird's eye, the amount of clear space that opened up in a thicket.

Anyway, this heightening of the senses redoubled his anguish, because the world around him was not a happy one. His sharpened perception of all the tints and contrasts of external life only highlighted the decadence, transitoriness and secret stress that wore down society and nature, whose apparent harmony barely contrived to cover, with a light varnish, the ever-present threat of collapse.

Even in this state, he told himself, life was worth living. He was drawing close to the time when he must take up his daily routine, his salesman's office, his numbers, papers and phones, and his only excursions would be shopping trips for bare necessities.

In the afternoons he walked along the lake and sat on the lawn that reached to the shore under an uncertain sky. In a state of puzzlement he clipped his fingernails. His mouth had a salty taste.

He didn't dare distance himself from his surroundings, much

less extend his walk to the wood on the opposite shore, where the figure had not reappeared. He realized that, somewhere along the line, he had reached a feeling of intimacy with the apparition—he who had hardly ever achieved intimacy with anyone. The photo, which he had stopped carrying with him, keeping it in a dresser drawer, was only a reminder that once there had existed an old lady by the name of Alicia Lastre who in a moment of idleness or vanity had decided to immortalize herself, alone in her armchair, before a camera's dispassionate lens.

On one of those peaceful dusks, at a far end of the lake, Natán leaned against a rock and stroked a cat's compliant head near a houseboat that appeared to have been abandoned by its owners, whom he had never seen. The floating home had been moored on that spot ever since his arrival at the apartment—a crude wood affair held in place by a flimsy dock that seemed, like the craft itself, at the point of collapse, or so its rotted-through planks attested. The water, in its to-and-fro, moved the house gently about, weakening its fragile structure. Birds had made their nests on the fractured roof and were perched on sills whose windows were kept open with badly rusted hinges and nails. Ducks were hobbling about in the doorway.

That afternoon, as the cat was having a snooze on his lap, Natán, immersed in the silence, recalled the moment of seeing his father kiss a heavily made-up woman on a park bench, when quite suddenly the cat jumped down to the grass and started making sounds that seemed to resonate in his inmost being—noises that were more than simple meows. The animal's body contracted and the hair on its back jutted out like a fan. Natán sat up in amazement.

From a corner of the houseboat, leaning on one of the damaged beams, the man who looked like Natán's father, the same as the one in the photo, was gazing at him quite severely, with eyes impenetrable as stones. He took off his hat and threw it into the water, where it sank like a piece of lead. A gust of wind caused the houseboat to shake. The man, with a sure step, turned round and went for the dock. Natán was startled to see the broad shoulders, deliberate stride and head of white hair. The man crossed over the gangway without looking at Natán, who did not move his eyes from the unperturbed figure. The ducks took off into the air, quacking. The man stopped, ran a hand through his hair, then kept walking calmly over the rotted planks. When he got to firm ground, he turned in another direction—rather than coming toward himself, as Natán expected—and went along the muddy, stagnant water.

"José! José! I know it's you!" Natán cried out and made some halting steps.

The other continued on his path without turning around, bending a bit and lowering his head as he moved among the trees that were lit up by the setting sun, walking on the soft grasses, nearly stepping into the waters that were gently lapping against the plants by the shore.

The birds on the reddened surface of the lake kept as still as marble figurines until a flock of quails took to the air, formed ranks and crossed over to the forest of pines. The man passed along the hedges that surrounded the squatters' houses and disappeared into a thicket.

Vainly did Natán, standing by the houseboat, wait for a gesture or sign of recognition. Night was closing over the landscape. A chilling moisture came up from the rippled lake, turning the breeze into an icy breath. The cat rubbed up against his legs and made whining, lamenting noises.

Natán's first impulse was to make for Teresa's apartment on the second floor, and only when he was ready to knock on the door did he remember that Teresa no longer lived there; she had taken flight from him, had abandoned him, perhaps because she had loved him beyond reason or because she had wanted to put a stop to this phase of her life, so full of sadness or disgust or shame. At that moment such explanations were no good at all; the only important thing was that she was not there to be a refuge for him, nor was anyone else. He found, hanging in a window, a scrawny Christmas decoration that struck an incongruous note. In the building's hallways he could not detect the slightest sound or the vaguest human presence—as if all the tenants had decided, like Teresa, to get out. In the parking lot below, the cars were inert, lifeless bodies. On the ceilings, cobwebs were sagging from the weight of their useless fabric. Shadows all around him enlarged the trees.

As soon as he got to his apartment he turned on all the lights, to uncover whatever traps the furniture might have laid for him. Then he ran through his worn-out address book, where he came across names he didn't recognize, and names of others who had long ago moved from Miami, or people who had broken with him over political differences, from envy or jealousy or mere indifference, and names of people who had died—like José's aunt—and he came to realize that one of the very few friends to whom he could turn was his old university buddy, Antonio; but Antonio and Gloria were not at home, and the telephone's ringing resounded in vain. For a second he was tempted to call his ex-lover Sandra, but even in his anguished state he felt he hadn't the right to look for her after he himself had forced their breakup.

He dialed the home of Gabriel Perdomo's family and asked to speak with the man's mother, who in the past had shown him some consideration. On hearing the woman's kindly voice, he started by telling her of his visit to her son at the clinic in Naples; then he said he would like to speak with her in person, that very evening if at all possible. After some hesitation—a bit tremulous, but fully courteous—she agreed to see him and told him how to get to her place. Her home was near the water in Key Biscayne, one of Miami's ritziest neighborhoods.

Before leaving, Natán had another look at the photo. Alicia was still by herself, but in back of her, in place of José Velázquez's standing figure, there appeared a kind of white spot, or a cloud with a light sheen.

To get to the Perdomo family house, he needed to cross the entire city. He felt he had no time to lose and decided to overrule his usual aversion to highways, for his urgency was greater than ever now that he had seen close up—not in a photo but in the flesh, and with irrefutable clarity—the face of his half-brother.

Indeed, it was he. Who else could it be? In whatever form, angel or demon, enemy or friend, this was his brother, the son of his father, tied to Natán by the indissoluble link of a common origin. And what was more, his appearance that afternoon had stirred an intense feeling in Natán, the kind of thing you could only explain in terms of blood ties; for the presence had awakened in him the type of joy or sorrow you experience on meeting someone you've known all your life, or someone you've loved, and who—due to a misunderstanding, a bitter exchange or a simple whim—has chosen to take a path in life different from yours.

He was now passing by those immense buildings in the city center, resplendent and cold, lit up with strident colors, jutting out against a hazy sky, enveloped by a murky mass of sea and by the latticework of bridges and freeways where dozens of cars like his flew along at dizzying speeds toward indeterminate points— or perhaps, he thought as his hands twitched at the wheel, toward impending, unforeseeable death. Milky blotches of clouds were threatening to submerge the tips of those tall towers. Between them floated a brightly lit advertisement, pulled along in a streamer by a phantom airplane.

Across the bay, lights from boats and buoys bobbed on black swells of water. Natán's route over the water took him past deserted beaches and mangrove swamps; then he paused at the first traffic light on the key to get his bearings. After a few turns he found the Perdomo house, which was indeed a mansion. He faltered before getting out of his car. It was not the opulence that scared him; it was the fear of behaving erratically in front of strangers. He took a deep breath, like a swimmer before a plunge. He felt out of control.

Gabriel's mother had decked herself out for a gala reception: formal hairdo, full makeup, fancy dress, perfume, jewels. Perhaps this was just her way of facing the world, Natán thought when she opened the door. All those cosmetics and adornments could not mollify the impact of age; her fifty-plus years were apparent in every line of her face, which was fully reminiscent of Gabriel's, just as José's face reminded him of his neglectful father.

And this lady too, with her cosmetics and artifice, gave the impression of a neglectful mother—or so it seemed to Natán when, after an exchange of greetings and smiles, she led him through a succession of stately rooms toward the terrace, where she said they might be more comfortable.

In that respect, she had hit the mark; for as they sat right by the shore with its ever-present swish of water on rocks, enveloped in darkness, each of them could barely read the expression on the face of the other, which Natán—and most probably the lady—considered a kind of protection.

"I don't know how to thank you for your kindness to my unfortunate son," she said as they sat down. "What can I offer you to drink?"

"Nothing, thank you."

"I'll make it myself. The girl has just left. She said she had to see her mother but I think she's gone to see her boyfriend—that's how young people are today! Tell me what you would like. How about a whisky?"

"No—really—nothing. What a beautiful house this is!" Natán said, thinking of Gabriel's letter and his contempt for his family's wealth, the "Midas touch" that turned everything into hateful money.

"It's a good house, but I prefer the one we used to have in Havana. Aren't you also from Havana?"

"I'm from everywhere in Cuba. My family was always moving here and there."

"Cuba! I never thought I could live so many years away!" the woman said. "If you don't mind, I think I'll have a little vodka. Can't I get you even a glass of wine? I would feel better if you kept me company."

"Then please bring me an apple juice."

After taking her drink with gusto, Gabriel's mother said, "I must tell you again how thankful I am...."

"You've nothing to thank me for," Natán broke in. "The truth is I'm not mainly interested in your son—although of course I feel for him in his illness—but I want to be honest with you. As I told you on the phone, I am interested in getting news about my brother, who was a close friend of Gabriel's. That's why I went to Naples, but the people at the clinic wouldn't let me talk with him."

"They didn't let us, either. They say it's part of his therapy, to keep him in isolation for a while. I think they know what they're doing, and I trust the doctor who's handling his case. If only you knew how much we've suffered, his father and I."

But in your voice I hear no suffering, Natán thought, and quickly said: "I can imagine."

"Do you have children?"

"No."

"Gabriel is our only child. Probably that's where we went wrong. We gave him everything a parent can give a child, we gave him whatever he wanted. We overprotected him. That could have been another mistake. You always wonder why."

Natán kept silent as the woman took another drink. With all her refinement, a streak of vulgarity showed through.

"Gabriel is an ingrate, a monstrous ingrate," she offered. "Excuse me for saying so."

Now the real woman is talking. "It's nothing at all," he said. "I understand you."

"You can't understand. If you don't have children, you can't possibly understand. We were so hopeful, his father and I. Please excuse me for saying this. I know you're a man with a good heart, because otherwise you wouldn't care about your brother. How old?"

"You mean, how old am I?"

"No, your brother."

"He's almost as old as I am, forty," Natán said, and paused. "My father—well, my father had him with another woman. But I love him as if he were my mother's child, too. He, my brother, is also a troubled man."

"What a pity. And how can I help you, Mr.—what did you say your name was?"

"My name is Natán—Natán Velázquez. And my brother is José Velázquez. Does that ring a bell? José was a very close friend of Gabriel's. I think they saw each other often."

The woman lowered her eyes.

"Gabriel's friends did not come to this house. What does your brother do?"

"Other people have asked me that question, and it's hard for me to answer. He didn't have a steady job, let's put it that way. For a time he sold used cars. My brother's aunt had Gabriel's phone number, and that's how I found you. That must mean José used to call here. You've probably spoken with him."

"I don't remember," the woman said, and got up to pour herself another drink at the bar in a corner of the terrace. She wobbled on her high heels, then sat down again and said, "You've been honest with me, so I'll be honest with you. Gabriel's friends had something to do with his downfall. I won't deny he's been troubled ever since childhood, even if he was always extremely intelligent. If I weren't his mother, I could call him brilliant to the point of genius. His teachers said it. True, he did have some psychological disorders. They started when he was a teenager. But his friends were the ones who got him mixed up with drugs, and that's what destroyed him. You can see why I didn't want to know about any one of them."

"My brother was different."

"I'm sure he was. There could have been exceptions. But since, for the most part, they were dreadful people, I told Gabriel he mustn't give this phone number to any of them—and most definitely they were not allowed to come here. In spite of that, some of them used to call. It's quite possible one of them was a certain José. Yes, I do think so."

"Did you happen to keep the address or number of any of those people?"

"I have an address. I don't know if it's a friend's. But I hope it's not your brother's. I have the address because, early one morning, we got a call from a woman telling us Gabriel was sick and we should come for him. It was a frightful place. When we got there, Gabriel was out cold on a rickety bed and the house was a filthy ruin, just horrible. We had to run him to the hospital, where they told us it was a drug overdose. He almost died."

"Who was in the house with him?"

"Two men and a woman. They looked like criminals. They even asked us for money. Think of that—asking us for money, at such a time! It was a nightmare."

"Can you give me the address?"

"If you think it will do any good. Is your brother also a drug addict?"

"I don't know. He disappeared some time ago and nobody, but nobody, knows a thing about him. I'm at the end of my rope."

"Well, I saved the address just in case. With Gabriel, one always expects the worst. I'll get it for you now. Are you sure you don't want some whisky or vodka? Or can I bring you some more juice?"

She got up and crossed the terrace with an erratic step. *She's a bit tipsy,* Natán thought, and it struck him that his coming here had been a piece of nonsense, like most of his recent actions; he'd come to the wrong place for help and company. The waves were hitting into the rocks with sudden snaps.

From behind a promontory flanking the house, in front of the gloomy sea, a man appeared on the slender fringe of sand that could scarcely be called a beach. Darkness concealed his face, but his masculinity was as easy to see as his white hair. He sat down with his back against a rock. Natán went to the edge of the terrace and was about to go down the stairs to the sea when Gabriel's mother called him.

"Careful! One of those steps is broken."

"You see that man siting against the rock?" Natán asked.

"What man?"

"There, on the sand."

"No, I don't see anyone. Look, here's the address. It's near Biscayne Boulevard, in the Northeast. I suggest you go there with someone else. It's a rough neighborhood."

"Are you sure you don't see that man? He's right there on the beach. Don't you see him?"

"No ... no ... I don't see him," she said, faltering. "Are you trying to scare me?"

Natán looked at her with contempt.

"You're drunk."

"What are you saying?"

"Nothing. Wait here a moment. I'm going to have a word with him."

Just then the shadowy figure got to his feet and disappeared into a mangrove swamp that skirted the shore.

"You're not going to make me crazy!" Natán shouted.

"Please leave my house," Gabriel's mother said. "Here's the address. Now, please go. I don't want to have to call my husband."

Natán put the paper away in his pocket and mocked her beseeching tone. "You are a drunken old woman. You don't love your son or anybody else. Gabriel told me you never stopped trying to buy him off. Why don't you just get him out of that hospital and let him live in peace!"

"Please, go away," the woman said, quaking. "I thought you were a decent man."

"It doesn't work to be decent with indecent people. You think you can manipulate everyone, just because you're rich?"

"Gabriel!" she cried out. "Gabriel! I'm calling my husband. Please go now. He has a pistol."

"I don't doubt it. Just keep on defending yourselves with money and guns. You won't go far."

"Gabriel!"

An old man in a kimono, quite out of breath, appeared at the terrace door.

"What's going on here?" he said in a voice both menacing and timid. The open kimono rather tastelessly showed a flabby chest.

"This gentleman is a friend of Gabrielito's, and he doesn't feel well," the lady said, at once moderating herself.

"I'm leaving now," Natán stated. "Please be so kind as to show me the exit."

"What seems to be the problem, young man?" the other man said, trying to project an image of strength. His eyebrows, nose and eyes were contracting and expanding.

"I have no problems, and I'm not young either. Now, how the hell do I get out of here?"

Cruising homeward on the jam-packed expressway, where other cars went charging past him at breathtaking speeds, Natán felt a heavy fluid filling his lungs and cutting into his breath. One of the tall buildings appeared all lit up in red; it seemed to be the color of blood. He remembered those lines of Keats:

That thou wouldst wish thine own heart dry of blood
So in my veins red life might stream again

Those words, he thought, contained a message directed personally at him, but he couldn't tell what it was. A passing truck let loose a current of air that blasted his car, and for a second the steering wheel was almost out of his control.

He got off the expressway at Biscayne Boulevard. He had decided to stop by that house where Gabriel Perdomo had had a momentary meeting with death. Not for the purpose of finding José—for he knew the time and place of that encounter were not his to choose. It was the other man, his brother, who would have the last word there. He, Natán, could only submit and hope. His own will in the matter counted for little; or perhaps, he thought bitterly, for nothing. In the meantime, until the other chose it, he should follow such impulses as happened to seize him.

Along the boulevard, prostitutes of both sexes, watched over by majestic palm trees, made inviting gestures at passing cars. Maybe he could take flight for a few hours in the embrace of arms that had grown accustomed to clasping strange bodies. He had two hundred dollars, or all his extant capital, in his pocket, but it wasn't worth the effort; he realized he was too preoccupied for a decent erection. Anyway, it was not escape he sought but, quite the opposite, remembrance. So he quickly passed by, deliberately ignoring those short skirts that revealed powerful thighs, those breasts standing out from low-cut blouses, those lustful motions that also revealed desperation, and those faces, lit up by lively eyes, that were more like masks.

The house to which Gabriel's mother had directed him was a tumbledown structure in a depressing neighborhood, rather close to the blind seer David. Among cracks in the ruined sidewalks, weeds were growing madly. Distressed fences gave no privacy; they only made a broad expanse of misery. Dim light from street lamps shone on deserted yards and doorways. No sooner had Natán stopped the car than two young black men came out of the house and approached him distrustfully.

"What you lookin' for, ol' man?" one of them said in singsong English.

"Either of you know Gabriel? Gabriel Perdomo?"

"You want some coke?"

"Gabriel gave me this address."

"Sure, we know Gabriel. Now, you want some coke?"

"How about José Velázquez? Do you know José Velázquez?"

"We know Gabriel, we know José, we know Juan and Pedro and Julio, we know everyone. Good Spanish dudes. What you like, man? You don't look like *po*-lice. What's your thing? Coke? Grass? Tell us. What you like? A lady?"

"No, I ..."

"How 'bout a man? You like a man?"

"Talk *respectful* to the man, Irving!" the other one said with a thin smile, his gold teeth gleaming in the half-light. "Do not worry, my friend. You are among good people. You can speak the truth, without fear."

"I'm a friend of Gabriel."

"We already know that. He's a good man, that Gabriel."

"I'm looking for another friend—José—José Velázquez."

"He's a good man, too. But neither one is here. You want to stay a while? Why don't we get down? We got a party inside."

"No thanks, I'm in a bit of a hurry."

'You seem a little nervous, man. Don't you want somethin' to calm you down?"

"We got the best coke in Miami," said the man with the golden teeth. "Thirty bucks a half-gram, fifty a gram, special price."

"No, that's not it!" Natán said, feeling his lungs about to explode.

"Don't tell me you came here for nothing, man. Don't worry. We're serious people."

"Fine, give me a gram," Natán said, starting the engine. "Now, when was the last time you saw José?"

"José? He drops in here every once in a while—smooth dude, very cool. Fifty dollars, my friend. If you give me eighty, I give you two. I'm in a generous mood. You won't find a better price anywhere in Miami."

"And you won't find better quality, neither," the other said.

The two had pressed their faces to the pane of the car window, which Natán had lowered halfway. With a smart movement, Natán managed to pull four twenty-dollar bills out of his pocket. One of the young men gave him a pair of plastic vials that looked like medicine.

"Come back whenever," he said. "We got plenty."

"Tell José that his brother Natán is looking for him."

"We will. And you come on back."

Maybe I'll try some, Natán told himself as he drove. *Maybe this will help me enter another dimension. Tonight is the crucial night. I need a change of direction.*

These thoughts came to him like living beings that took shape as other people's words. Flashing traffic lights appeared to show him a hidden passage—a journey governed by unseen rules. Neon signs were twinkling with anxiety.

A sudden, familiar voice from out of the night was telling him clearly, in a dry and authoritative tone:

"You wanted it this way."

"No!" Natán cried back, braking the car. "*You* wanted it this way."

"You, you," the voice answered.

"Go fuck yourself!" Natán said.

The voice was gone. Natán breathed deeply and floored the pedal. He was now in a hurry to get home—as if the anguish that had stopped up his breathing were a part of the car itself, and the unbearable suffocation would quit as soon as he got out.

In the dark of his home, he did not find the air he needed to breathe with ease. He turned on the lights one by one. He went to the bathroom and in front of the mirror he sprinkled some white dust on the back of his hand, as he had seen people do in films. He took two or three snorts; tears filled his eyes, and he sneezed. He couldn't recognize his own face, and every heartbeat vibrated in his ear like sound from an amplifier.

He went onto the balcony in a frenzy, wolfing down a piece of bread with marmalade. The figure was on the other side of the lake, just where he knew it would be—imperturbable, immobile, statuesque in his boldness. Natán snatched up the photo and ripped it into tiny pieces, which he sprinkled over the railing.

The poem. The command. The summons. He retrieved the paper he had crunched up in a drawer, went back to the railing and declaimed at the top of his lungs:

"This living hand, now warm and capable of earnest grasping, would, if it were cold, and in the icy silence of the tomb, so haunt thy days and chill thy dreaming nights that thou wouldst wish thine own heart dry of blood, so in my veins red life might stream again and thou be conscience-calmed! See? Here it is. I hold it towards you!"

He looked at the paper again and sat on the carpet. *A sacrifice,* he thought, and so it was; but how so? Should he give his blood so his brother might live? David the seer had asked if he believed in vampires. What was more, David had told him that someone wanted his blood. Natán stood up and wiped the glass table with a cloth.

That was all so old, he thought, feeling that such things dated back to another life, another time. *So old!* he kept up as he spat on the glass and used his spittle to clean it vigorously. *To give your life for another, for a god, for a people, for a brother. History is repeating and eternal. I am a particle in a river of blood.* He sat down on the floor and leaned his head against the wall, which had acquired a slight wavering motion. Yes, he was a speck of dust being pulled along by the arid wind of the unknown; an ant, a pebble, a man with no roots, no traditions, no faith or love, no essence.

"Bright star, would I were stedfast as thou art—" or so the other Keats poem went. Not him, though—he could never be steadfast, for his firmness depended on others, or perhaps on *the* other. He

himself was puny, a nothing, a cipher. He went back to the balcony and stretched himself out on the cold flagstones. His memories were as fleeting as the vapor that moistened the glass door. And so was he—a trace that would vanish, a puff of smoke dispersing.

But no! No! he thought as he got to his feet and ran to the bathroom, where he took stock of his flashing eyes in the revealing mirror. His mouth was fleshy, quite unlike the thin lips he remembered. *I am alive, my name is Natán,* he said out loud. His brother had no part in his life, because he was not of this life. *But which life?* he asked himself. To be sure, the spirit had no body— but then how did it appear?

He thought back to that young man in the hospital courtyard, the one with his wrists furrowed by gruesome scars. He got a knife out of the medicine chest and slashed his right arm. Then he cut himself a deeper wound. The blood flowed out in such a carefree manner that it could not possibly be the vital fluid on which his life depended.

This is a game, he told himself as he sat on the rim of the bathtub and watched the blood drench his shirt—*a game between brothers, a harmless game between brothers. I should go out and find him. I'll show him the wound. Aren't you my brother? I'll say. Everyone has told me how generous you are. Where is your generosity? If you can't treat your brother well, you can't treat anybody well. Do you see my blood here? It's the same as your blood—the same as our poor father's, who now has to die far away from his sons.*

But my father rejected me!—José would say.

And me too! Don't you realize he rejected both of us? But I'm not rejecting you. And don't you reject me! I'm ready to do whatever you ask. You see that, don't you?

He swathed his arm in a towel and left the place in a hurry. He descended the stairs in the firm belief that the moment of his greatest deed had come; but when he got to the edge of the lake and the dock of rotted planks, he felt a dull discomfort. The figure was still on the other shore, but now he feared he could not get close to him; he doubted the other would wait for him or extend a friendly hand. Even so, he felt he must run the risk of his life and try to get there.

He started around the shore. A sparkling moon lit up the surface of the lake, so still he felt he could walk across it, as if it were a resilient metal and not a treacherous, fathomless mass in which one could sink and die. The trees replicated themselves, down to the last detail, in that misleading mirror. From the grasses and shrubs, like an outcry, came the rubbing sounds of insects. Lizards and snakes were crawling along on the rugged ground, while spiders wove their fragile webs with a meticulous fervor. Flying fish jumped up from time to time, rupturing the luminous pane of water, and disappeared.

The branches joined together in a roof of twigs, a menacing structure. Natán had the impression of being at the edge of an island, of skirting a dark region from which he would never escape. Far from inspiring comfort, the landscape struck fear in him. The sentient life he had perceived in plants, ever since he had been a boy, seemed to have expired. Their immobility now looked more like death. He passed by the houseboat whose rickety frame shook helplessly—a shelter fit for stray animals or wavering spirits.

He came to the makeshift huts of squatters: distressed little buildings of cardboard and pieces of wood, topped with ill-fitting tiles or dented zinc sheets; hovels, dimly lit by kerosene lamps, to make him forget he was in America. From behind many crevices, Natán felt the gaze of suspicious eyes upon him. He quickened his step. He had heard that the inhabitants of the small, marginal neighborhood were mostly criminals, drug addicts, crazy people. Dogs began to bark furiously, sullying the stillness with their uproar. Clothes hanging on lines, whitened by the moon, looked unfit for human bodies.

A scream cracked the night apart. Natán was frozen. Then came another scream, and another; howls rising from the forest. An old lady limped out of a hut and stopped near a picket fence.

"What is that noise?" Natán asked.

"I don't speak Spanish," the lady said with a snarl.

Natán repeated the question in halting English. All at once, he seemed to have no command of that language.

"Some piece of trash who smokes crack," the woman said. "You see that house there, near the pine trees? People are smoking crack there, day and night. It's a horror. The police come and arrest them, and the next day they're there again, or others like them, and they just keep on, as if they had nothing else in the world to do, they're in shit up to their chins, disgusting and perverted little chickens. But you must know that. Don't you know it? You go up there, don't you? One of these days I'm going to get fed up and set fire to all that trash."

"I don't go up there," Natán said. "I live in the building across the lake. I couldn't sleep, and I came out for a walk."

"Then have a glass of milk and say your prayers," the old woman said. "If your conscience doesn't let you sleep, ask for God's forgiveness. And if you don't believe in God, you'd better kill yourself."

"Yes, at times I've thought about that," Natán whispered in Spanish.

"Grandma!" A child's voice was crying from the hut. "Grandma, I'm afraid! Please come!"

The old lady went back to the dwelling with her crippled walk, humming, scratching her back and shoulders, bobbing slightly. A pair of enormous cats came out to greet her, whining like children.

Silence fell over the tumbledown shacks, over the stagnant spot of water and the frost-bitten firmament. The dogs had quit barking; their very anger seemed to have subdued them. He waited for the screams to resume, but they did not. He moved to the water's edge and scrutinized the forest; in the denseness, someone seemed to be moving. Farther away, where he had seen the stranger foraging, a shadow leaned against a tree; but that might be a trick the moonlight played with the branches. After a few minutes' hesitation, he kept walking.

The house about which the woman had yelled was an abandoned cottage, largely destroyed by fire; the walls were blackened stumps encircled by rubble. That part of the structure which the flames had not visited was halfway overgrown by vines and other leaves that were slimy to the touch. On the other side of a broken window, a candle flickered. Natán put his face up to the fragment of glass.

A girl and two boys were sitting on a grimy floor, motionless and quiet, detached from each other, as if they were immersed in a ritual. Still young, they were emaciated and skeletal, which added age to their immobile features. A rotten odor of sweat and excrement suffused the room. The girl started crawling over cracked flagstones as if looking for a lost object; she moaned like an animal. After scouring the room, she stretched out in a corner with her eyes open. One of the boys stood up and looked around in confusion. His chest was covered with tattoos. Natán stood back from the window to avoid being seen.

A bit further on from the house, where the dense forest began to broaden out, he happened on another boy squatting under some shrubs and warming a tin can with a match flame. A heavy smoke was emanating from the can. The boy gave a start on seeing him, but instead of running away or even getting up, he stayed perfectly still, squarely meeting his gaze, and then voraciously inhaled the smoke. In the light of the moon, his look had a wild glow.

Natán kept moving, abashed at having stumbled into the private ceremony; and for a moment the image of that boy's curly locks, juvenile beard, demented look and delicate, womanly eyelashes, quite a lot like those of the suicide or fake suicide Tim Harris, made him forget he was scouting this forest and lakeside in search of his brother.

The dogs had begun barking again, with real energy this time, as if someone were egging them on. Natán plodded along the muddy shore in soggy shoes, dodging puddles, pulling apart thorny shrubs, waving away brazen insects, feverish and losing breath. Across the lake, his apartment building was completely dark except for the lights in his own rooms. Was he seeing things, or was someone strolling on his balcony with folded arms? The idea crossed his mind that he had been the butt of a nasty joke; he filled up with an insensate rage. Then he had a second look, and plainly no one was there; only the outline of the folding chair where at other times, lazy and peaceful, he had sat in the sun. *The time of my innocence,* he told himself. He stepped on false ground and was suddenly in water almost up to his knees. The tall grasses were camouflaging tiny bays; if he wanted to keep walking, he must enter the forest. His arm was now ablaze in pain from the wound.

He was hard-pressed to make his way through the thorny thickets and rough undergrowth, at times having to step around huge piles of trash, which in the darkness appeared to be projections of the earth itself. Moistened tree-trunks and misshapen branches were colluding immorally to block out light and air, providing shelter for all kinds of vermin whose busy life could prosper in the shadows.

Every now and then, in an effort to find his way through the labyrinth of plants, he cast his eye up above the treetops into the starry sky, cold and remote, which he could only see in fragments. Nocturnal birds were warbling out of tune, weeping quietly or laughing inscrutably.

Abruptly the thicket ended, as if broken by a spell. He had reached the clearing in the forest that he had seen from his balcony. Never would he have imagined it so vast, a silent meadow lit up in blue, enclosed by a wall of trees, its grasses resplendent under the full moon. In its center was the corpse of a truck, covered with dew, sprouting patches of grass and moss that had penetrated its shattered windows and had overgrown the rusted body. Remains of decapitated birds piled up on the hood—victims of ritual sacrifices—gave off a frightful odor.

Natán crossed the clearing, looking in all directions; he could feel a human presence nearby. On one side, a translucent fringe of pines yielded him a diaphanous view of the lake, and of the shore that the one who lay in wait for him had haunted; but now he could see only the tall grasses beside the water. A cat sniffing around some large mass took off at a dizzying run when Natán came near. The mass looked familiar; clearly, it was a body.

Stretched out on the grass, with short hair drenched in a dark liquid, her face disfigured by blows and body cloaked in a ragged dress, a woman was motionless, maybe sleeping—or was she too still to be asleep?

Natán touched her shoulders, her bruised forehead. He didn't dare touch her left breast, erect and pallid beneath the rags, to see if she had a heartbeat, but after a few moments of hovering over her with a lover's tender concern, he saw there was no need; she was dead.

His first thought was that his brother had murdered her, to show once and for all his malevolent nature, so everyone might see it. A crime without motive was the supreme display of cruelty. Natán got to his feet and looked around, waiting for the other to appear. A cold breeze came running through the forest, shook the branches and leaves, and stirred up a plaintive rustle.

But no! It could not be José who had committed such an act. Natán unwrapped the towel from his arm and wringed out the blood, which seemed to be not his own but the woman's. A pain-filled spasm shook him from hand to elbow. Then again, maybe José had done it; or so Natán thought as he put a few uncertain steps between himself and the corpse. Perhaps he had had to choose a victim, and this perfect stranger had fit the bill for a necessary sacrifice. In other words, the woman had died for Natán himself. Such things did happen. Didn't the history of wars and holocausts prove it? But no! His brother would not have let himself be drawn into violence, even into violence that had an occult meaning. In the middle of the field, the broken truck was gleaming like a solitary animal taking a nap in the grass.

He crossed the brilliant bluish meadow and went back into the woodland, leaving behind the lake and the body of the unknown woman. In the midst of the thicket appeared a path, festooned with plants whose frigid touch recalled human flesh emptied of life. A bird cried out sharply from on high in the pines; another answered more softly, as if to placate. The dialogue resounded with crystal clarity in the black foliage. A pronounced odor of basil rose up from the moistened earth and spread itself in a heavy mist. The leaves made crunching noises under Natán's hasty step. No more was he glancing about himself, nor did he even lift his head. He had but one adamant goal, to get away as fast as possible; and he fixed his eye on the end of the sylvan pathway, where the airport's lights were twinkling.

After a long march he emerged at the road that skirted the runway. Innumerable red and blue lamps were blinking on the flatland, where planes were at rest like gigantic, sleeping birds. Flags deployed from lonely towers wafted in the meager breeze.

From behind a curve came a pair of blinding headlights. The car approached at full speed, then halted with screeching brakes. A man in uniform bolted out with his pistol waving toward the innocent sky.

"Freeze!" the man shouted at Natán with a threatening gesture.

Instinctively Natán darted away, letting fall the towel he had been using as a bandage, and jumped over the high fence that separated the road from the runway. The policeman screamed again with real force, but Natán was already running breathlessly on the asphalt, under the sleeping wings. He was in a frenzy of blind motion, stumbling, slipping on patches of oil, propelled by an animal's fear, and was about to hide behind a rolling stairway when his pursuer grabbed him and pulled him to the ground.

Natán fought back with all his energy, raining blows on the other man's chest and prying himself loose from the other's heavy arms, but the man grabbed him again, and vainly did Natán fight against that body which seemed to be made of metal; the intense pain in his arm forced him to yield.

The other man kept beating him, screaming, "You son of a bitch! You fucking son of a bitch!" Natán bit him savagely on the shoulder and spit on his hair, but a slap on the face calmed him down. The man pushed him to the car and threw him onto the seat as if he were a parcel. Stunned, and while the policeman spoke by radio with other patrols, he managed to grab a handkerchief out of his pocket and fix it on his wound, which was bleeding profusely. He leaned his head on the seat and closed his eyes. He thought of Tim Harris, who had supposedly bled to death, and a faint hope began to take shape inside him. His mind could see through to a clear and open space. More and more he felt free of his anguish, and at the end of an exhausting journey.

Random words he could hear—"bleeding," "madman," "woods," "behind the lake," "airport"—had nothing to do with him; nor did the deafening wail of sirens that filled the air. He was quiet when they put the handcuffs on him.

His loss of blood had removed him, lifted him to a weightless place where nothing, no one, no person or spirit could follow. Only when the police car took to the road, followed by the boisterous line of other police cars, and passed by the edge of the forest and lake—now plunged into a solid darkness, as the sky was covered over with clouds—did Natán register that he had completely failed in his objective. Somewhere in the distant shadows, where he lay in wait, the instigator had foiled him again, without ever coming close, without letting himself be known, aloof and mysterious, hidden and untouchable; a wily fugitive who had trumped him one more time, or perhaps, he thought, for all time.

CHAPTER

ELEVEN

From behind barred windows of tinted glass, which dimmed the light and colored the landscape in shades of violet that gave a false impression of tranquility, Natán looked out at dawn on the empty city that bit by bit, as the sun rose, filled up with vehicles turning impulsively here and there, like rides at an amusement park, driven by figures whose silhouettes, viewed at a distance behind wind-shields, were hardly human at all.

His cell was on the seventh floor of a jailhouse that rose up, smack in the center of the city, like an embarrassing bulge.

The summer had seemed rather boring, like a gradual descent on a long slope; but then came the precipitous fall to unseen depths and the abrupt feeling of an irreversible decline, making the last five months a season unique in Natán's forty years.

Now, sitting on a bunk-bed next to the huge, barred window that had been densely built to withstand gunshots or blows, he was peeved at the appearance of those huge constructions housing wealthy banks, or hotels where empty-headed tourists stretched out on their terraces with drinks, sucking up the sun with an indecent greed; and even more was he disturbed to see, across the water, a vast complex of hospitals whose windows mirrored the one from which he now looked out on this ahistoric city—an urban mongrel on a southern flatland hastily thrown up to receive refugees who could never belong anywhere.

Was he pining for his own past? No, he didn't think about the place of his birth, where amid hope and euphoria, as well as profound suffering, he had reached his manhood; he didn't hanker after that dead-level country where he had read his first books and had come to know love; he had no nostalgia for those sparse and poorly made towns, for cities where people lived and died beset by indifference, quackery and the bitter humor that goes with laziness and fear—for the island that most of his fellow exiles reverently called their homeland.

Homeland: the word, in Natán's mind, stood for a set of experiences that had drawn him, across time, to his present situation: that of a prisoner waiting for breakfast at a jail in downtown Miami.

At home, too, he had lived in tight, crowded jail cells, as well as in larger prison quarters filled up with men who had lost any sense of manhood or humanity; he had slept on floors carpeted with feces and urine; he had marked on a wall, with desperate scribblings, the passage of days until he had covered the cement with lines; and he had watched, beyond thick-set prison bars, the endless dawns and dusks that lacked any relation to his life.

The difference was that, in his youth, he had gone to jail for following an ideal, for rebelling against an order he considered perverse, denouncing the lies and hypocrisy behind a so-called system of justice; while this time he had been a victim of circumstances. It was as if the time between his prison terms had simply pushed him into a void where he could not control his actions, where destiny was a force that kicked him around at will. And the feeling of being at the mercy of unseen elements only sharpened his sense of decline.

His cellmate had been released the day before. He was a weak-bodied, sickly man, with large and bony hands that had one time squeezed his wife's neck a little too hard, but not hard enough to prevent her from taking him to court on a charge of attempted murder. His story, Natán thought on recalling it with some envy, had been so simple: the story of a man who had stopped being loved, or more likely had never been loved at all. Natán, by contrast, had been loved quite a number of times, though in an incidental, incomplete way. At day's end, these encounters with love had not brought him satisfaction or peace; rather, they came down to the memory of a fragrance, a stain on his pants or bed-sheet, a senseless refrain crooned on a rainy night or a phrase once pronounced with feeling and then repeated in a farcical tone.

Through five months of jail he had heard lots of stories, a good number made up, but all possessing a kernel of truth that bespoke the same thing: the desire for power, for domination, for material things, cars, money, drugs, or for human beings, for people whose love or sexual favors had become indispensable to an aggressor who then embarked on an act of violence. Plentiful, too, were the sordid tales of vendetta around smuggling, fraud, betrayal and blackmail; as well as crimes in families, over politics, or some esoteric ones around race and religion.

And he? What was he doing here, living with strangers behind metal doors, with time frittered away in repetitions of empty formalities; in rooms that couldn't be compared to Cuban cells, but were no less malignant? The quickest answer he could give himself was that he had gone crazy.

Undeniably, he had suffered an acute mental crisis that had

climaxed in the events leading him to prison; but his memory was consumed by the man, the name, the presence who bore conclusive responsibility for his stay in this cell.

Still, he had his doubts. Looking out at the city that had been built up with impeccable logic—streets of perfect design, modern urban transit rails, drawbridges that gave way for cargo boats and luxury yachts—he wondered whether indeed he had been the victim of an external circumstance and not of a dark impulse that had started and grown inside himself.

He had damaged his own situation by blurting out, in a most inopportune way, that he had killed a woman in the forest. Handcuffed in the police station, faint with weakness from his wound and a policeman's blows, then subjected to a brutal interrogation where he admitted to violence against the police and possession of drugs—they had found almost a gram-and-a-half of cocaine in his shirt pocket—he had somehow felt compelled to add: "I'm also a murderer."

That word had changed the officers' double-dealing expressions into ones of almost euphoric surprise. After a pause in which he had tried to catch hold of some fleeting thoughts, Natán, strumming his knees with his fingers, had described the corpse lying on the bluish meadow in that lonesome clearing.

"She was a prostitute. I killed her. I didn't know what I was doing."

"How did you kill her?"

"I beat her. I don't remember it very well. I would rather not speak about it. I feel weak. I need to sleep. May I have a glass of water?"

The police cubicle, with its brilliant, implacable lighting, had seemed an extension of the dream in which he had been immersed since that afternoon, when he had seen at close range the man on the houseboat, a figure at once familiar and alien. Later he remembered that, in confessing to the officers, he believed he was sacrificing himself to save his brother, whom he considered the actual murderer. He also remembered that in telling his tale, he had felt himself, for the first time, to be a hero, to be fully free, as if the self-incrimination that might cost him his life was also redeeming him. Later, when they took him to the infirmary, he repeated to himself:

"I saved him. And I saved myself too. I saved myself from him, from everything. Now I can be at peace."

In the days after his confession, he was possessed by a ceaseless exaltation, and the most trifling details of his limited routine were imbued with vigor and resonance. The daily prisoner count, the rasping sounds of prison doors opening and shutting, the hours in front of the TV screen—where he thought he saw his face go by—the cold insides of his prison cell, the antiseptic folds of prison sheets and towels, the movie-picture vistas of life through prison bars and windows, the incessant chatter of fellow prisoners who had no room for silence, the very scar on his arm, all paid silent witness to a transcending act of courage that he would bring to completion. His nights were set on fire by dreams of sumptuous feasts, women made for pleasure, dazzling landscapes. When he awoke, he did not lament misfortune as did everyone around him. He knew he had fulfilled his mission. If anyone had asked him about his mission, he would not have been able to answer, for at bottom he could not say what it was. It was not a thought but rather a feeling. When he brushed his teeth, he hummed a trifling melody that he had overheard on the prison guard's portable radio. At times the brushing caused his gums to bleed, and he was fascinated to observe, in the mirror, his lips spattered with red. The image brought something to mind, but he wasn't sure quite what.

Soon enough, the relentless force of justice delivered him from self-incrimination. In two weeks' time the true killer showed up—a drug-dealer who was also an addict and a pimp, and who had nothing to do with José, with the spirit-world or with free-floating fantasies. The woman, it turned out, was a vicious, unhappy soul who had tried to play a dirty trick on her executioner. These details came from the defending lawyer, paid by Natán's boss, who had never believed a word of the confession. Natán's heart went out to his poor employer, who took charge of selling Natán's car to cover his mortgage for a year, exactly the length of time he had been sentenced to jail.

In the end, the penalty had fit the crime—even with Natán's insolent behavior during the trial, his clumsy attempts to be convicted, his refusal to go free on bail. And the sentence had even been reduced to six months, five of which had already passed.

Now, pacing in his narrow cell, gazing at the sun's progress across the cityscape, sitting gingerly on his bed or on the other bed that until yesterday had been occupied by the man who had lost at love, he wondered whether his yearning to stay in jail might be due to his need of punishment, or to the fear of being free to face, one more time, the figure or phantom he had identified as his half-brother.

He hadn't seen him since that night in the forest. Vainly had he looked for him in every cell, every hallway, every room through which he had passed, including the courtroom—even spying for him among pedestrians on the city's faraway streets. In vain had he hoped, or feared, to see the face that was easy to spot in any crowd; but the man who had changed his own life had apparently returned to the void without leaving a sign.

And Natán continued wondering. He wondered whether he had been attentive enough at those moments when he thought he had seen him; whether the voices he had heard, and then ceased to hear, had only been the recollection of other distinctive voices that had taken shape through a trick his memory played on him. However, he told himself, Gabriel Perdomo had dreamt of José and given Natán a message from him. Teresa had seen him in the photo standing by his Aunt Alice; and then the apparition had begun stalking her. Gabriel had gone hopelessly mad, Alicia had died and Teresa was only a name, an image of a loved one who had become part of his disappearing past. The photo's fragments, which he had scattered into the night from his balcony, had probably, by now, dissolved into earth and water—an idea that gave him a certain comfort.

Just then a guard opened the door, his country bumpkin's face distended in a yawn that showed indifference to the prisoner. It was time for breakfast. Natán took a tray from a metal cart and walked with bowed head along a corridor that went in a circle around the gigantic room, while other prisoners were coming out of their cells. The common prisoner's uniform couldn't manage to make lookalikes of the many dozen men whose faces Natán well knew: faces young or old, black or white, expressionless or beckoning, sad or good-humored, which Natán observed askance— for staring was inadvisable—as the men made their way to the tables.

The din of conversation, of jokes and occasional insults, rose all around him, begetting a chaotic mass of English and Spanish sounds to which he added not a word. From the start of his prison sojourn, he had decided it was pointless to speak. At another time and place, language had served him for asking questions, expressing feelings, declaring opinions or making complaints; while here, aside from the brief and cordial hello, he had nothing to say. While staying in a cell with others, he simply let them talk among themselves; and while sharing a room with a single man, as had happened for two weeks until the day before, he contrived to play the listener's role whenever the other looked for a conversation, only inserting brief comments in order not to seem uninterested or rude.

After breakfast, the first meaningful time of day—the others being lunch and dinner—the prisoners could go back to their cells or stay in the large room to talk or watch TV. Some had actually taken to that life. For Natán the most severe consequence of prison, apart from the obvious lack of liberty, was its tedium. He, who fled from the society of the others, from their swaggering and their aggressive posturing, delighted in the fact that for the first time since his imprisonment he had a cell all to himself; and he hurried back to the refuge of those walls that had become a protective shell for him.

Many prisoners filled up the emptiness of the hours by writing overlong letters, hunched over their stationery like artists finishing a masterpiece, drawing every letter with the same intensity they'd used to commit their misdeeds. Natán had no one to write. Surely his father was dead; and even if not, what difference did it make? At first he thought of writing to Antonio and Gloria, his only friends, but he was ashamed to tell them he'd become a prisoner. Only his boss, to whom the police had spoken after Natán's arrest, knew of his situation, and Natán had asked him not to tell anyone. Then, after the man had twice come to visit, Natán had asked him not to return, for it depressed Natán to speak across the window in the visitors' room.

Bars and windows kept him apart from the world, from life—if only in a formal sense, because he knew what was out there. He knew the streets of Miami by heart, he had been a visitor to New York and Madrid, and of course he had spent most of his years in Cuba. Then again, one always hit up against those bars and windows. He didn't kid himself. Cuba, for him, had been the worst of all prisons; while the freedom he had sought—which must be some amalgam of peace, happiness and personal maturity—eluded him everywhere.

Still, the notion of suicide, the impulse to end it all that he had felt in the months before jail, had disappeared; death no longer beckoned to him. People killed themselves, he had read somewhere, because they expected too much from life. He, however, hoped for nothing and desired nothing—perhaps because he had perished inside.

As a child he had wanted so many things: above all the love and acknowledgement of his parents, neighbors and schoolmates. As a teen he had wanted the love of God, and then the love of women. As a young man he had wanted to free his country from the oppressive regime that controlled it; then, in his disappointment, he had wanted to forget his beginnings and his past. Most recently he had wished to get close to his brother; and this desire too, like all the others, had in time turned against him.

Now, alone in his cell, standing near the window, he felt suddenly overcome by an irresistible insight, cold as ice and cutting as a razor's edge. The radiant morning lit up the most elusive places of the city he had chosen as his permanent home. He pressed his forehead to the bars and tapped his fingers on the glass. With his entry into prison, the supernatural part of his thinking had given way, bit by bit, to a naked skepticism as gross and unavoidable as his own body, with its pressing needs and petty desires.

In his third week of jail he had seen an old man die of a heart attack at a meal. The bones of fried fish were gleaming on the man's plate when, in a mortal spasm, he knocked over a chair, spilled a glass of water on the table and fell to the floor. Two months later, an effeminate young man stabbed his lover while they were watching TV in the main room. Both times, the bodies had instantly turned into flaccid objects: waxen dummies that gave no reactions. And he himself had groped that woman's bluish skin in the forest clearing; he had peered into half-open eyes that shone as expressively as pieces of glass.

If his brother was dead, as everything seemed to suggest, and if his corpse had been like those Natán had seen, he could hardly imagine that his supposed inner spirit would afterward have taken bodily form to hound and frighten him.

It was true that at times, lying on his bunk-bed, as he listened to his cellmates tell, for the n-th time, the story of some exploit— a perfect robbery, a tremendous fight they had left victorious, an artful scheme they had played on some sucker—he felt himself being watched; but then he ascertained with a rapid glance that the men in the cell were paying no attention to him, which led him to guess that the invisible presence must yet be haunting him. At other times a new prisoner or guard, seen from a distance, bore a startling resemblance to José Velázquez; but closer up, the resemblance vanished. Such things occurred less and less frequently, and Natán was surprised to find himself thinking of his brother as an unrealized possibility, whose time to take solid form would probably never arrive.

On this September morning, just a few weeks away from liberty—or rather, he corrected himself, from leaving jail—he looked out on sidewalks drenched in sunshine, where pedestrians kept up the futile work of moving themselves from one place to another. The sight of some youngster led him to reflect that José, too, had once been a youngster; and that at night, in Cuba's sweltering heat, he and Natán might have shared a bedroom in one of the many houses their father had rented during his incessant flight from himself; they might have drawn Chinese shadows on the walls, or terrified each other with stories of beheadings, or fought

over a toy or a book, as brothers do. On the crowded thorough-
fare below, a young man nervously dodging traffic recalled to Natán
that José had been a young man, and that the two of them might
have squandered their leisure noontime hours flirting with girls in
parks or on streetcorners, or spent all night drinking with rowdy
friends on Havana's Malecón, or even plotted against the regime
in a ramshackle house on the city's outskirts and ended up in
prison, after a trial at which the prosecutor would have crudely
and bluffly declared: "The Velázquez brothers are guilty of having
tried to overthrow the eternal government of the people"—and
they would have looked at each other with a secret pride. Years
later, perhaps, they would have taken the path of exile. Perhaps
they would have lived next to a lake where they fished for nimble
trout that would meet their destiny in a frying pan. Perhaps they
would have fallen for the same woman, whose love they would
have chosen to renounce in order to preserve the bond between
themselves. Perhaps they would have grown rich and renowned.

But life was not a might-have-been; or so he told himself as he
made for the small prison bathroom. On the wall, the man who
had gained release the day before had written: "My wife is a slut."
That was the man's truth; and Natán felt compelled to record his
own. That same afternoon he wrote: *The dead are dead. Outside
this life, there is no life.* Then he lay down to sleep until dinnertime.
He dreamed that a cat was whispering questions in his ear, while
scratching the pillow with razor-sharp claws. Out of the pillow
came photos of faceless people. When he awoke, Natán could not
remember what questions the animal, in a lovely feminine voice,
had asked.

During the meal he did not take his eyes away from the TV,
where a pair of fugitive prisoners went falling down a slope while
being handcuffed to each other. Their exhausted faces showed an
unbreakable will to escape and also to stay together, quite apart

from the handcuffs that kept them forcibly joined. It was an old film that Natán had seen in his childhood. Did one of them die at the end, or did they both live? He couldn't remember. He went back to the cell, where he lay down on his bunk to look up at the ceiling. It gave him no cheer to stand at the window and watch the town fill up with nightlife: headlights making the streets brighter and brighter, illuminated buildings, neon signs. From his bunk he only saw the sky glowing with the cool radiance of urban frivolity.

With a sudden clang, the cell door opened and a guard was telling him: "You have a visitor."

Natán got up without enthusiasm and followed the guard through a labyrinth of corridors.

Just as I was at peace, he thought, having to quicken his step to keep up with the guard who was walking very fast and, apparently absorbed by being in charge, scarcely paid attention to the prisoner. Natán figured his boss had come to visit again, despite his repeated statements that he wanted to see nobody.

At regular intervals electrical doors were opened and closed by uniformed men looking out from glass cabins. Closed-circuit TV screens glistened in the corners—a show of efficacy for the modern judicial system—while bland voices requested or gave instructions over invisible speakers. Natán and his custodian passed along a bar grille behind which a group of prisoners had gathered round a priest who was giving a mass. Two of the men were on their knees, taking communion. The priest was saying a prayer in Latin, and his hands shook as he parceled out the ritual wafer. It occurred to Natán that those primitive rites, born in the Roman catacombs, had come twenty centuries to be repeated in catacombs of the present day.

Finally the guard led Natán inside a cubicle, and before he knew it Natán needed to lean on a doorway in order to remain on his feet. On the other side of a glass wall, a smiling woman was anxiously fixing her hair.

"I'm so glad to see you," Teresa said. Her words came into the room over an intercom that slightly distorted her voice.

"How did you find me here?" Natán asked, approaching the glass panel with halting steps, like someone walking on a minefield.

"A woman called and told me," the fluttery voice came bounding toward him, without seeming to originate in those quivering lips on the other side of the glass. "She didn't want to tell me who she was or how she got my number. She told me you were in this jail, and she gave me the address. Then she hung up before I could even thank her."

Natán lowered his head. He couldn't bear to look into his lover's moistened eyes, or see her mouth contorted by emotion.

"It doesn't matter to me what you've done, it really doesn't matter," Teresa said and began to cry. "I'm not going to stop seeing you." She dried her tears and asked: "Who was that woman?"

For some moments Natán kept silent, trying to track a furtive thought. At last he said in a low voice: "It was probably a girlfriend of my half-brother. She called me one time, a few months before I came in here."

Teresa's visage brightened up.

"So you finally got together with him!"

Natán carefully placed himself on a chair that looked weak and unsteady, no match for his weight. All at once, his entire life seemed to depend on his ability to sit down.

"No, not exactly." He took a risk and looked Teresa full in the face. "It seems he's still traveling. How are your girls? And your husband?"

"Everyone is fine. I might divorce, I'm not sure. I'm at loose ends. I have to apologize for having left you that way, so suddenly, without giving you a chance."

"A chance for what? You did the only thing you could. Seriously. You've no need to apologize."

Teresa shook her head.

"If I hadn't left, you wouldn't be here."

"Do you think so, Teresa? I'm not so sure. You know, just this afternoon I was thinking in that tense, in 'might have been.' But the might-have-beens aren't real. What's real is what was, or is."

"You don't seem so happy to see me."

For the first time, Natán smiled. He said, "I just have to get used to the feeling."

Natán put his hand on the glass, and Teresa brought her face close to the crystal wall.

CHAPTER
TWELVE

When he had completed his first prison term in Cuba, Natán spent some days wandering around Havana before going back home, where his mother waited for him as she read her Bible or breviary, stirred the soup in a half-century-old pot, or sowed coriander seeds in her lizard- and ant-infested yard. Frankly, Natán preferred to spend those first days of freedom living intensely, rather than hurry back to his bland and boring town in the provinces. Just so his mom wouldn't worry, he sent a telegram telling her to expect him in ten days.

He was twenty-two, and his expulsion from the university for political reasons, culminating in a six-month prison term for keeping in his room a pair of books by a well-known Soviet dissident—a fellow student having informed on him—awakened his desire to be a rebel, to carry off daring and unusual projects, even if he couldn't quite say what those were. Soon, and easily, he was memorizing poetic works by García Lorca and Miguel Hernández.

He was chewing his fingernails and masturbating three times a day. He felt a tornado's energy inside him.

His father, now remarried and living in the capital, had refused to see the son who had blasphemed against his political credo, but had sent him money through a mutual friend. Natán spent it in frightful bars and restaurants near the portside hotel where he slept past noon. From his crumbling balcony he watched the procession of Greek and Russian sailors, besotted and often in the company of mulatto girls who looked around them to make sure they weren't being followed. Ships with rusty prows went sailing by on the dark, oily bay. Natán descended the staircase of broken steps, counting out his precious ten-peso notes.

When his money was gone, he went back to the country on a rickety train that stopped at every insignificant station. Plans to launch conspiracies were swimming in his head. His angst was heightened by the locomotive's whistle, which sounded to him like an urgent summons to change the world.

The second time he left jail, after a three-year stay for writing a draft of political reforms—the co-authors being two friends, one of whom also turned out to be an informer—he still harbored the adamant will to live freely. An amnesty had opened the doors of exile to him. He imagined the act of beginning again in a foreign land as a heroic deed; and he wrote out feverish declarations. He went down on his knees before his mother and asked her to come with him. The old lady, swept away by the extraordinary gesture, said yes. At that instant a cat jumped in through the window, knocking over a container of stew and rice. After the shock, mother and son began to laugh, and Natán's important scribblings went into the trash can.

Now, as he rode the highway in Teresa's car, breathing the air of dusk for the first time in half a year, he could feel his vital energy beating inside him, but fragile as a piece of string one could snap in two without trying.

Teresa was talking nonstop. Three days earlier, she had taken her kids and moved into her mother's house, and nervously she wondered whether she would be able to break it off with her husband, who had rained blows on her breast and face after hearing she'd visited a man in jail. Natán went in and out of listening. It looked as if the city had expanded during his confinement. He could gather that Teresa was waiting for a marriage proposal, but in his convalescent state he resorted to an insecure silence as a way of postponing things. Violet-coated clouds were coming apart on the far edge of the sky where the sun, with huge, fiery flashes, was vanishing among the roofs and trees of distant neighborhoods. The air smacked of salt, and Natán imbibed it greedily.

Teresa slowed the car down; traffic in front of them had stopped. Something had happened on the right side and cars were changing lanes, which created a severe bottleneck. Minutes later they were passing by a pair of cars that had become a jumble of metal, ringed by ambulances and police vehicles whose harsh beams were swirling in the dusk like lights at a festival. The screech of a siren lengthened into a lone, interminable note. On the pavement lay two bodies, covered with white sheets that stood out starkly against the black asphalt. Natán could see how still the fabric was, clinging to those two inert forms.

"How horrible!" Teresa mumbled.

They were both silent for the rest of the way to Natán's building.

The dark inside of the apartment was suffused with a reeking humidity, the smell of must. Teresa ran to open the sliding door and the windows. Natán sat down in the living room with his back to the terrace in an expectant attitude, like a guest in someone else's house. Teresa, moving nimbly, dusted the furniture, shook out the mats, put books and clothes and other things in order, happy to channel her uneasiness into the task.

"We should eat," she said when she was done. "I'll call up and order us a spread."

"The phone might be disconnected," Natán said.

"I paid the bill two days ago. You owe me a pile of money," she laughed and kissed his hair.

"We can marry if you like," he said in a flickering voice. He noticed that the ceiling had been damaged by water leaks and would have to be repaired.

Teresa kissed him again. "Don't worry, we have time to talk about those things."

They made love rather clumsily, like people desirous of giving their best but afraid of not being able to produce the magic that had drawn them together at another stage of life, when they had brought themselves to the act with ardor and innocence. And vainly did Natán await the presence of the shadowy apparition that had watched their last sexual encounter, in this very room.

Afterward, from bed, Teresa talked on the phone with her mom and girls. She had decided to spend the night with Natán, and she promised that on the day after she would be there early to take the girls to school. For the first time he noticed her peculiar accent: traces of Madrid, unusually mixed with melodic highs and lows from the easternmost province of Cuba. She was a traveler like himself, and also like him she had learned and unlearned languages and customs, ways of speaking and living.

At dawn the roar of an airplane woke him up; without shoes he went to the balcony and leaned over, trying to remember what he had dreamt. A dense mist was covering the lake and forest. The airport lights, under a murky and tremulous halo, were shining weakly through the false clouds. The hardly visible trees were like effigies wrapped in a luxuriant gauze. A corner of the houseboat seemed to have vanished into the water and the whole construction was tilting recklessly, like a craft about to sink. He went back to the bed and stretched out alongside Teresa, who sleepily touched his forehead as if to make sure he didn't have a fever. Soon he was sleeping again.

He dreamt of a time when his parents were young and together. The two were dressing in front of an enormous mirror where Natán was also visible, but his childish body at times faded away, as if the mirror were a crystal sheet of water where the wind made ripples, disturbing his reflection. Father put on a wide tie that became a serpent and went slithering, harmlessly enough, among the combs and powder compacts on the dressing table. His mother was applying a gold-colored polish to her cheeks.

"You can't go with us," Mother said to Natán. "You can't."

"I don't want to stay by myself!" Natán cried.

"Don't pay attention," Father said, making a fine part in his hair. "He'll get used to it. Everything we've done with him has been useless."

"Useless, useless, completely useless," Mother repeated as she vehemently rubbed the makeup into her face.

Natán went into a room that looked like a cell, whose walls were covered with obscene words in impeccable handwriting. After a while his mother opened the door; alongside her was a boy with white hair and lips of striking redness, apparently painted.

"Don't you want someone to take care of you?" Mother asked.

Natán angrily shook his head. The other boy started to speak, clearly and fervidly, in an incomprehensible language.

"And don't you want someone to take care of?" Mother asked Natán.

Without speaking he fastened himself to the wall, trying to cover the dirty words with his back, and they stuck into him like pinpricks. Mother and the other boy knelt in a corner and started praying in unison, in that strange language; then they got up, brushed off their knees, and withdrew without looking at him, their faces quite hostile.

"You'll regret it," Mother said, shaking the bracelets on her arm with a menacing jingle.

Natán hurried out to find them and came into a backyard full of weeds. At the rear, a storm was severely shaking an already doubled-over tree. Near the roots, Mother was stretching a white sheet over the other boy, who was lying in the grass quite motionless.

"No!" Natán screamed. "Leave him alone!"

She covered him from head to foot as she whispered, like a litany, "Useless. Completely useless."

Natán woke up shivering. An emaciated light made the shapes in his room even more fleeting. He turned on the lamp beside his bed and got dressed slowly. Teresa mumbled: "What time is it?"

"I don't know. It must be about six."

He crossed the room sleepily, rubbing his eyes, dazzled by the light that came streaming through the windows. The twittering of birds and singsong of roosters made limpid sounds in the dreamlike silence.

"Is the sun up?" Teresa asked from the bedroom.

"Almost."

He opened the balcony door and took in a plenitude of clean, clear air. Fleshy leaves, branches and creepers, crisscrossed by delicate cobwebs, quivered under the weight of dew. The mist dispersed, and the breeze opened the view to a landscape whose colors unfolded without hurry: the withered green of vegetation, the whitish blue of water. The varied shapes, ephemeral and glowing, seemed to shift, moving blindly until they found their place. In the distance, earth and clouds converged until they were interchangeable. Bit by bit the light established itself, white, vaporous, confirming the lines of the trees.

At that moment, in the hazy and liquid distance, a man stepped out from among the pines and paused at the swampy edge of the lake. Natán leaned on the railing without taking his eyes away from the unmoving figure that seemed to be observing him. The man raised his arm and waved. It was utterly simple; no rejoicing, no fuss. The man waved again. Natán lifted his arm. Above the ruined dock, a gull described circles in a defiant, cunning flight.

Teresa, wrapped up in a blanket, went out to the balcony and said, "I'm cold."

"Go back to sleep. It's still quite early."

"Do you know that man on the other shore?" she asked as she encircled his shoulders with her arms. "I think he was waving to you."

"No," Natán said, "I don't know him."

But he was lying. He knew very well who it was.